SECRET PLANS
AND BETRAYALS

SECRET PLANS AND BETRAYALS

Book Two of
The Colors of Magick

Victoria W. Morrow

iUniverse, Inc.
Bloomington

Secret Plans and Betrayals
Book Two of The Colors of Magick

iUniverse books may be ordered through booksellers or by contacting:

iUniverse
1663 Liberty Drive
Bloomington, IN 47403
www.iuniverse.com
1-800-Authors (1-800-288-4677)

Because of the dynamic nature of the Internet, any web addresses or links contained in this book may have changed since publication and may no longer be valid. The views expressed in this work are solely those of the author and do not necessarily reflect the views of the publisher, and the publisher hereby disclaims any responsibility for them.

Any people depicted in stock imagery provided by Thinkstock are models, and such images are being used for illustrative purposes only.
Certain stock imagery © Thinkstock.

ISBN: 978-1-4759-4031-2 (sc)
ISBN: 978-1-4759-4032-9 (ebk)

Library of Congress Control Number: 2012913105

Printed in the United States of America

iUniverse rev. date: 11/08/2012

Contents

Dragons

On silver dreams I await you over,
quiet places hidden in green clover.

The ruby red fire and evil within
the blue wings of ethereal skin,

A golden dream of every lover,
shadow dark drones it over.

Fighters and warriors all dance to the tune.
Are they worth fighting to their doom?
These are the dragons of all colors;
some are good, and then there are the others.

By
Victoria Morrow

Acknowledgments

To Brian Cox—Without his expert counseling on fantasy "The Glen" would never have been created, as explosive as it was.

Frank Bosworth; my editor, my friend and also author of many books; my favor is "Never Play Leapfrog with a Unicorn."

Thank you all for your support and well wishes during these trying times.

Prologue

Odysseus sat on a corner cushion in Myst's new domain. The others were recovering from their current ascent from the caves beneath Aries' palace. Through keen eyes he watched them, his thoughts went through all that had happened. He now considered his potential powers. Could his magick protect them from the evils he had seen on this quest?

The quest started in an effort to save Myst from her marriage to Aries, King of the White Sands. But she loved Alex, Prince of the Palace of Mist, and he loved her in return. Odysseus's views ran back through all the events and difficulties they had encountered along the way. 'Who was responsible for all the traps and why?' He twisted his beard tighter in reflection. 'Alex had brought this on himself.' The wizard smirked; 'Alex had no right to promise his sister to Aries in marriage.' A year passed since Alex left and not knowing that she had given her heart to another man and vowed to wed him. Nathanial, the new Captain of the Guard and happened to be Alex's best friend. Therefore, when Alex arrived home, he was taken aback by this new information, and the fact she carried his child only turned the knife. What a mess he'd made between these two realms.

Odysseus's eyes then swung towards Myst. There was the fair peasant maid who could not bear to see Alex in pain and, foreseeing an impending war, she had gone to great magickal lengths to save his reputation and his Kingdom. Myst and Alex had grown deeply in love, even so, she had selflessly taken matters into her own hands by arranging to take Vickie's place as Aries' new Queen. He should have foreseen this connection between Myst and Alex. Instead, he had simply dismissed the tugging of something out of balance and had simply swept it from his mind. Odysseus felt the pain between Myst and Alex as she suddenly disappeared at the grand ball. He saw this glittering wristlet, but not before Alex. It was then Alex decided to start a secret group of unlikely characters to rescue her from the clutches of Aries, even if it meant risk of war.

Finally, after many trials and mishaps, the group found a way into the caverns beneath the tower where Aries had incarcerated Myst. The group now faced their final challenge. There, in front of them, stood a slimy staircase spiraling up into the interior of the tower where they hoped to rescue Myst. A magickal tower which was protected with a violent wind inside the turret. The stairway pummeled by a gale force wind, somewhat like a cyclone. The only way up seemed to be up the staircase with nothing for handholds and a beating wind which beat them with sharp objects.

After an overwhelming battle, they managed their way to the top. It was then they met a timid apprentice named Lotus. She had been learning spells which Odysseus was quite surprised to find a simple apprentice learning such a fearful spell as these with foxglove plus more. He took in the last few moments of their meeting, his mind running through everything that had happened up to this point.

Odysseus remembered his first sight of a very exhausted Myst as she collapsed in Alex's arms. She looked so fragile and frail. He overheard Alex whisper into her ear of his plan to save her. Now Odysseus was worried as he remembered that doomed feeling in his gut when she looked into Alex's eyes and whispered the soft, gentle words, "I, too, have a plan."

CHAPTER 1

Plans to Make

While the group performed greetings and the tales of their quest together, Odysseus took this time to use Myst and Lotus's work surface. At first, he was unobserved and took the liberty to look through the books she had recently worked on. If Myst had a plan then she must prepare in special ways, such as an out-of-the-ordinary potion or incantation. He pulled out quite a lot of parchment on empowerment, grounding, summoning and notes, but nothing signified learning of her plans. He investigated the close-by jars of spider webbing, different fungi, powders and foreign mixtures of all kinds. They all seemed carefully measured out by an intriguing balance machine, and then carefully funneled into each jar. These jars then aligned from east to the north. He pondered at each one, wondering why the impact of this strange placement. What was she up too?

He was almost complete in his exploration of the desk and prepared to explore somewhere else, when his eyes looked up to see Myst's head suddenly swung in his direction with great inquisitiveness. Seeing he had just been caught, he quickly leaned back away from the table with haste, as if a small school boy, looking around as if nothing was out of place. Myst make a quiet exit, and made her way towards him.

"What are you up to my friend" she asked? Scanning her table for any telltale signs of mischief and finding none, except for his small nervous twitch of playing with his spectacles, which he only used when reading. She leaned over the table across from where he sat, hands laid out upon the smooth tabletop with fingers spread and looked directly in his eyes. "You are up to something and I wish to know what it is."

It was then Odysseus's head suddenly jerked up, and in a whisper, "But if you would have told me of your feelings involving the two of you, we could have managed something . . ." Odysseus trailed off at her uncertain look. The issue was becoming uncomfortable and Odysseus took another path, straight to the point.

Myst was surprised when he calmly stood, leaned close to her and whispered, "Such as how you plan to leave this place? Or, for that matter, your secret rendezvous with Alex all this time without my knowing?" He had her there—she had never lied to him, she just never told him everything and they all had the right to be informed. In her defense whispered quickly back at him, "But why this quest, why did you not talk to Alex and explain I had to leave to save him and his palace from certain doom" she asked of Odysseus with a tired look?

"Alexander not only felt your loss, Myst, but he blamed me for the betrayal he was feeling. Alex thought we planned together and between us wove a spell so powerful Aries would take you over Vickie. Then you left that glittering bracelet behind only to give him hope and encouragement." Odysseus became angry at the thought of Alex finding Myst's little trinket. "Alex still does not trust me fully and, after all these years, it hurts me deeply."

"It must have slipped off when I threw the disappearing powder. I did not intend for him to find it." Myst looked deeply into this wizard's eyes and there she saw the pain he endured, of Alex even thinking of his own wizard betraying him.

"I heard you tell Alex of a plan. I wish to know it now!"

"Lotus has proved more than an apprentice; I believe her to be quite the mage, for I have seen her do more than a simple apprentice can do; and since we do not know her true heritage I think we have made right choice. She has studied hard and even taught me many new talents of dispelling evil and vile things." Myst finished in a whisper and looked over towards the group to see Willow had now noticed they were apart and would be investigating soon. Sure enough, Willow excused herself from this animated group of fascinating tales of the forests, to make her way towards Myst and Odysseus. It was not long before she too was part of the group of wizards and 'The Plan'.

Willow, Myst and Odysseus were well into a heated debate over Lotus's capabilities. A plan was now forming in great detail, and about the high risks to them all. Odysseus was always serious and meticulous in his work as he warned them once more of the perils of such a quest. In his mind, he was already mapping out the course they must take to make this mad and unwise strategy. His dispute was the linking of Lotus with a golden dragon and therefore breaking the delicate balance of the code of natural ancestral history of crossing an earthbound element with a dragon (unknown) element. It was a treacherous and unsafe game they played to make Lotus become a powerful Sorceress for their own achievement. Odysseus thought this a dangerous plan indeed. He almost hit the rafters when Myst told him of Lotus's involvement with Belisma. It did not help when Myst told him Lotus had learned her talents from Belisma as well.

"Then the plan is off! We cannot trust this girl! Have you all lost your minds? To mix a fire element with a tainted and vile elfin, is unquestionable!" Odysseus was not finished. "Then to mix those two elements with power of three light magick is pre . . . pre . . . preposterous," he stuttered!

Willow came to question him now. "How is it you come to know Belisma is Elvin in the first place and why do you assume Lotus is of his kin? She has told me of being taken from the forest when she was but a child."

Odysseus turned to his tiny daughter and gave a shrinking look. "Willow, how are we to know this to be true and not just a ploy to gain your innocent trust?"

"You may not know your own daughter, but you should trust in my talents by now and I say she is pure of heart, my Lotus, if not we would all not be standing here!" Myst spoke a little louder than usual and immediately hushed by the other two. "And if I say she told me of being taken against her will, I trust her." With a sigh, Myst gathered her wits and continued with the 'The Secret Plan'.

Lotus noticing her name filtering on a wisp of the breeze moving toward the group to join in this meeting, only to meet with Odysseus' hand stopping her cold in her tracks. Odysseus still steaming at the thought of her being evil; simply froze her in place. There she stood, immediately froze, as if a statuette. She did not even open and close her eyes. Lotus was now in an instant fog of confusion as they continued to argue over the risks.

Myst and Willow continued to listen with rapt attention. Odysseus noticed Myst sliding a glance to Alex for this attempted rescue, hoping all would be well, and as if he felt her gaze upon him, Alex nodded his approval. Myst smiled back at his relaxed position. Sitting in front of the fire, chair tipped back, as if there was not a care in the world.

'Smug,' was the word that came to Odysseus's mind, as he cleared his throat to get Myst's thoughts back to his plan. Odysseus was wise to leave Lotus out of this plan; he had no patience to argue with her about it. Also, with her having no clue of her soon to be transformation, he thought it best.

Willow and Myst, knowing Lotus and her shyness, looked at each other and nodded in same mind as Odysseus. Plans now placed in perfect order.

Alex found a carved box of cheroots and offered one to Nathaniel. "These look like a fine way to pass the time, as well as this full bottle of aged honeyed brandy; should we really allow these treasures go to waste?" Alex poured a small glass of the clover-honeyed brandy, clipped off the end of one cheroot and handed it to Nate. Nodding his appreciation, Nate accepted graciously.

"What about me?" Vickie stood there in a huff.

Spyder stood as well, "Aye, me too! Don't we get some of the fine stuff as well?"

Alex turned towards the two of them and started "Because I said so! I being your older brother; and you, my boy, are too young . . . go play or . . . or something." Alex ended this with a stern look at Vickie and reached out to ruffle Spyder's hair. Spyder did go off to play with a frozen Lotus. Vickie followed to keep him out of any potential danger, though perturbed she had gone from an adventuress to a babysitter.

Odysseus did notice Vickie batting Spyder away from Lotus. The whole time Lotus was frozen he had been playing the jester in front of her, making faces and dancing, finding it very amusing she could not move, as if captured in stone. Vickie reminded Spyder how apprentices were powerful beings, how Lotus would not be frozen forever, she would remember his childish antics and how she could turn him into a frog with a simple snap of her fingers. Odysseus smiled in amusement at Vickie's statement, only to see Spyder's face fall. Spyder then fell to his knees, apologizing profusely.

"Excuse us, Spyder, for we have much work to do," Odysseus said. While they carefully walked a zombie looking Lotus. Spyder's eyes popped out when they walked to the edge of where the rest had climbed the turret, held hands, making a circle and then slowly floated out and off the edge, descending into the darkness. Odysseus chuckled, "Well there is something Spyder will be stuttering about when we are back up".

CHAPTER 2

Transforming Lotus

Odysseus walking to a secret stairway he found earlier inside the tower, opened it, and wheeled out an oversized barrel full of fruits and vegetables. "Willow, my dear, you knew Sarpeden could not work on an empty stomach. You always had a soft spot for creatures of any kind," he teased, touching his finger on the tip of her nose.

"When I felt your existence in the palace and saw the omen of the red dragon's life as it slipped from its body, I started collecting food from the kitchen." Willow smiled up at her proud father. "I did not have the power to put the red Dragon to sleep as Belisma could and was hoping you could overcome this dragon's evilness."

Sarpeden was indeed astonished to see the four of them walk into the cave with a large wooden barrel overflowing with sumptuous looking food. "I am famished and was dreaming of the scent of fresh food. I do not recall the last time I partook of such an extraordinary feast. The grapes and vegetables are a wonderful change considering the ugly creatures I managed to capture. Being a golden dragon of magick, I have no palette for real meat and find it difficult to kill and eat any living creature." Sarpeden finished as she tipped the barrel using her front claws. In a sitting position, she downed the last of the fruit and its juices almost hitting her large head on the upper limit of the cavern. With a jarring slam, Sarpeden replaced the empty barrel on the cavern floor; it was an unpleasant thing to feel the earth move beneath one's feet like the quaking of the earth, making you feel quite small and insignificant. She chuckled as she wiped off the remainder of food and juice, "We must get me out of these caverns before I grow too tall. I shall be crushed slowly until death."

"Sarpeden do you know how long dragon's are thought to be extinct, or how we interacted with each other? Odysseus asked. "Why some live to be older or not have any powers at all. Long ago, magick came into play with some of us mortals, making us different from the rest. Even I live a longer life than many as a wizard, and I had to earn trust among the many as their protector. Many are still in hiding because of observable deformities that claim them as magickal people." Odysseus rattled on as Sarpeden tried several times to respond, but was only cut short with the interruption of an additional string of questions.

"Halt-You are draining my strength and sapping my sensitive brainpower," Sarpeden abruptly shouted, as she covered both sides of her head as if in pain. As her outburst echoed down the corridors of the cavern, everyone, but Odysseus, approached her, apologetic of his eagerness. He explained how magick looked through the eyes of the skeptic now and being judged by whom you were and the color of your magick made you good, neutral or vile. If indeed neutral, then you were, by design, judged as easily to go evil at any given moment.

Odysseus promised to explain further when they had more time. Right now, they had a plan to put a new Queen and love into the palace and Sarpeden calmed with eagerness to hear this grand news. The wizard gazed into the dragons eyes and saw she was holding back information, but for now he promised they would have more time later. He remembered reading about different dragons, their domains, whether they were evil, good or a little of both. Golden dragons, even though fire breathers, were wonderful swimmers as well. Eventually, she would be able to breathe fire, this was the risk that Odysseus warned them all once more of the risks they were about to partake.

The thought came to him how he must go to the shrines and learn of all of them, their powers, their intelligence and more of his own powers, it was obvious dragon's lived after all this time, but how? Were there more and if so where are they—and are we all in danger to come? Odysseus told Sarpeden of their agreed plan; they were to transform Lotus from apprentice to Sorceress using all of their combined magick. Odysseus noticed Sarpenden's confused look towards him, the whole time, even she knew this plan was not promising, even with their combined magick. Odysseus looked toward Myst in trust hoping with all hope she was accurate in the fact Lotus was already mage material. If indeed this is a mage to begin with and very strong willed, then all would be well. But if Belisma had indeed corrupted her in any way this could turn her the other way, making her a terrible adversary to contend with and indeed unstoppable.

Combining all their powers, plus his devotional ring from Delmar, the powdered heart of a red dragon, it just might be achievable. Odysseus now knew from Myst how Lotus had indeed 'true love' for Aries. Lotus would have to fight off the small amount of evil which would try to taint and lure her to the dark side. There was much good inside her, but enough guilt, because of Belisma, to contaminate her. Lotus must truly, without a doubt, be filled with love for Aries for this to work.

Sarpeden prepared for any plan these wonderful humans had contrived to save this palace. She wished for her own escape from this dark place, but after that quick discussion with the Elvin wizard, she was anxious about the people, would they attack her on sight? For what they did not know or understand; they feared. So Willow whispered quietly in her ear.

"What was that about, Willow?" Myst could not but ask.

"Sarpeden is afraid and so I promised her a grand home, where she could fly and be free," Willow replied. "I had to calm her."

"And where is this grand place?" Myst asked, with raised eyebrow.

"Home, with us, of course. I was thinking of this wondrous pond and I told her of a palace that would welcome her with open arms as protection." Willow smiled at Myst and shrugged her shoulders until their attention was drawn to the wizard. Myst wondered what Alex would think of taking home a new pet.

Odysseus prepared his one vial of potion. With mortar and pestle, a request for forgiveness, and sharp quill, he pricked the finger of each participant of this task. For the first ingredient was a drop of blood of each person, including Lotus and Sarpeden. He approached this golden dragon with caution. It was not an everyday occurrence, drawing blood from a creature such as this. Sarpeden noticed the wizards approach. Knowing what was needed she decided to make things a little less tense, as she pulled back one of the small golden scales to reveal the tender hide underneath. Odysseus winced as he drew blood from this gentle giant and watched in fascination as it dripped gold and fizzed as if acid as it dripped into the bowl.

Sarpeden healed quick, as if it never existed. Odysseus then sat, ever so careful, with his bowl of blood, for this was a one-time chance from the ancient past. All watched enthralled as he sprinkled a small amount of the red dragon's blood, as well as what he called his midnight oil from another vial. Odysseus chanted over the small bowl as it fumed, fizzed and occasionally bubbled over in several different colors. Finally, he swirled it until it was smooth enough to pour into a clean vial. Now was the hard part, for Lotus was to drink it immediately. With minor struggle and a gagging noise, she drank it down. It looked and smelled like clover honey; clearly, it did not taste like it. All knew the risks and were willing, they nodded towards Odysseus.

"We are ready," was all Myst said, and this propelled the chain of events.

Odysseus walked a still confused Lotus; he reached for her hand, seeing honey potion swirling in Lotus's eyes as he walked her close to Sarpeden who already had her golden wing spread to receive Lotus containing her within its warmth. Lotus now wrapped within this dragons wing with hope and love; all was ready.

It was then Sarpeden saw Odysseus slip on a ring of silver and dark stone. "What is that ring, Sir Odysseus and what does it do?" Sarpeden asked.

"Now is not the time, my Dragon friend, we must do this before the potion wanes," he answered.

"It must be of vast significance, for I remember seeing a draft of that same ring; maybe not exactly the same, but close. Belisma was looking for that ring, teaching the red dragon to hunt for it and to annihilate its owner and all around him or her who possessed this ring. I think, Odysseus, your life may be in danger as well as those who are close to you," Sarpeden told Odysseus. "I now fear for you; Belisma wants all those rings at any cost."

"What is so important about this simple looking ring?" Sarpeden asked, an already knowing look in her eye. "He also had a rock or crystal of the same type, only in a different setting, so there is no mistake."

Odysseus was becoming perplexed as he pondered on why Belisma would need this ring or even know of it. "We shall discuss this later, of rings, rocks and where you came from, but as of now, we have much to do. Concentrate, my friend of gold," he instructed, as he finished placing Delmar's ring on his finger. "All of you, concentrate." They all held hands with Odysseus and Myst on each end placed their free hand upon the treasured Dragon.

At once, they felt the sudden surge of power run from their very being, up and through their spines from the very earth itself and contain in their being. The ring was holding all powers for use and they must do this transformation now. The others sensing urgency rushed to focus on their visions as per instruction. The room stood still in time and place, but for a moment, then the sudden channeling of minds began with a shock to their beings.

Visualizing a golden light which passed from the very earth, through their bodies and out through their hands. The ring used as an extra enhancement of power, clearing all blockages and amplifying the energy that now passed through the wing into Lotus.

It was working, they could feel it as they visualized harder in incredulity as the dragon glowed and shimmered in gold from all their efforts. They heard music from Odysseus's ring singing out as a Fey Flute would in a song of love and peace. Music that would calm the most savage of beast, but only a small amount of time passed before Sarpeden and the rest started feeling the rapid energy drain of their own power as well.

As a whole, they saw magickal doorways, which now seemed to be opening. They slowly, as a unit, un-locked each entry, and for the first time they stepped inside the novice psyche. This magickal group suddenly felt the understanding washing over them of the more delicate intricacies of a magick mind weaving an epiphany of the highest caliber. Weaving their thoughts throughout Lotus's brain using their special talents of love, understanding, and protective forces from any evil influences, each one was now taking a different path.

Myst, concentrating on Lotus's love of Aries, could now only be with him through the loving good they passed through her.

Odysseus focused on the negative energies, fears and secrets she held, and for an instance, it was an intricate and problematical door to find and open. This small child had sacrificed much to be close to the man she loved. He was in the process of mending that hatred when, being overcome with a wash of exhaustion, as if Lotus intentionally slammed the door closed on him, breaking the chain. He staggered back away from her breaking the chain they had formed.

It was then, now totally drained of all their power, they fell. Odysseus pulled away just in time; for they were lost in her problematical mind and time had passed rapidly.

If not for Myst shutting those doors, they all would have lost time and become drained of all their complete powers. At his break of letting go of hands, the force of Lotus's new power had thrown them away like leaves on the wind. Odysseus, unaware he had been thrown clear of all power, lay in a heap far across the cavern where he had slammed into the rocks and rubble. Knocking him into complete unconsciousness the moment he hit, he now followed a firefly through a tunnel of darkness, but to where? Myst crawled in exhaustion and laid his head in her lap, running her hand through his now growing white hair. "He breathes," Myst croaked out to the rest, "but needs much rest."

Sarpeden told her to let him dream of his past. The dragon would lead him down a path needed to claim his right of who he really was. Myst watched in fascination as his hair grew longer and whiter, wondering at his dream and would he ever tell her about this past, which he obviously had suppressed over so many years and how Sarpeden knew of dreams.

Odysseus eyes focused only on this golden bouncing light, which spiraled through an endless tunnel until it exploded into his past world. He was once more a young boy growing up. His life exploded before his mind in a vivid and fast-paced blur. Odysseus was back in time when he lived in the Dark Shard City.

CHAPTER 3

The Dark Shard City

Odysseus was back in time inside 'the Dark Shard City'. He had studied their history of how this city came about. At first it was a dismal and barren place for the punished Cel'eset's, they were thought of as 'the Fallen Elves', committing some form of crime or another in the social order and therefore banished from their people. Driven from their homeland, one by one, these fallen elves left behind their belongings, families and everlasting feelings.

There were enough 'Dark Elves' now to become a community. After trudging across the rough forest land, away from the Cel'eset's encampment for many miles. They finally found a place to call their own. They decided to create their own community, and called upon the elements in their plight. They followed an unusual humming sound deep within their forest without thought or reason, started to dig out their new city. Here they found an amazing and astounding amount of crystals that would hold them safe in a haven in which to live. The people had to dig and raise magickally the elements of the dark obsidian, translucent crystal from the depths of the dirt and rubble. These dark crystals soaked the warmth of the sun and retained the heat for the nights. Within the hollow of a new forest, these Fallen Elves called this new village "the Dark Shard City".

Now the decision fell upon this new society on whether they were to remain a band of good or evil. Upon many long and heated debates, most Elves decided on the good side. Then again, there would always be a handful who constantly disagreed, saying it was they who were thrown away from their families and lost their positions. It was these people who stood, lurking in the dark, biding their time. There was one powerful master, who wished to remain evil and practice his dark arts alone, 'Racknar'. It was this Racknar, after many years of building, saw to it the new appointed their first King and pressed to choose a Queen to stand by his side. He also made sure that this King was very young and very pliable in his hands at the time. Racknar also made sure his first wife had no powers, but beauty was all a young man needed. So he found a beautiful woman named Annabelle. They wed immediately, and she was soon with child . . . She never knew the greatness of this city for she died giving birth to her daughter; under mysterious causes.

Everyone remembered the one fateful day, a worker brought forth an irregular globe found deep within the shards. The new King not knowing what this odd shaped object of beauty represented, mistook it as an artifact of hope for the future and the life source of their new city.

Odysseus studied this artifact whenever possible, for its origin its shape and purpose.

When Odysseus's parents found he had special gifts beyond their control, they left him, as an only child, amongst many strangers to begin wizards' school. Of course, the school had been the Dark Shard, dark and lonely.

The King of this city, however, loved and reveled in its beauty during the day, watching the sun as it bounced off every tiny peak and crevice. Nightfall, however, became a problem, as his beautiful sparkling city seemed to sink within the shadows of the night like a mythical citadel. Even glowing candlelight could not penetrate the walls and show his wondrous city at night. He tried fairy light and it could not penetrate the sheer walls. Not being a King to give up his ideas, he called upon his magicians.

Numerous attempts were made to light this fascinating city, as the magicians used all their powers to create just the right potion. They worked late into the night, stirring, boiling and even using radiant ores procured from faraway places and under curious circumstances, for no one dared to inquire. The King walked to their tower with his daughter, Daphne. They gazed upon these magicians' feeble attempts of glowing cobwebs, lanterns and ornate glowing objects. The plans, crumpled parchment, scrolls, potential preparations, and saw the discord in which they worked, all to no avail.

On one occasion, when visiting the wizards' towers, the princess Daphne noticed one of the wizards gazing at her with a perplexed frown on his face. He started to approach her warily and she noticed he was not really looking at her, but only curiously at the shining blossom she always wore in her hair. At this wizard's proximity, she took a step back in fear behind her father, afraid of what he would do to her. Her father stood tall and assured her all was well. She knew, in front of her own father, they would not dare harm her. He was right, of course, as she poked her head around him, the wizard only showed interest in the blossom.

He stopped the others in their work and simply, with an old crooked finger, pointed to the common blossom. This particular flower only grew on a near hillside; Daphne called it her 'Moon glow', for it opened only at night and closed tight during the day, as if to hide from the sun. 'Could it be that simple?' the wizard's thought. They scattered immediately, leaving a very confused King and Princess, who was now without her ornamental flower. These magicians left the city and scoured the forest for this vine, bringing scores of them back to their tower and within a short time they had come up with a plan; asking for secret audience to see the King and his daughter. The magicians carried into a small chamber a very large and tall pot concealed by a heavy, dark and mysterious material. They asked all candlelight be extinguished, making the Princess very ill at ease, for she was not caring for the darkness. The King, awaited as the candles were snuffed. Then one of the wizards brought forth a glowing orb and tossed it into the air where it hovered above them all. It took on the shape of a full moon glowing down upon everyone within the chambers. The chamber lit up at this display of magick and Daphne came out of her hiding place to witness what would transpire next.

The Princess could not believe her eyes as the wizard who had approached her earlier removed the heavy veil. With slumped shoulders, she sighed, for it was simply her favorite Moon glow flower, as it wound around a trellis. Then, when the wizard removed the glowing orb, her eyes became wide as did the King's when this plant opened its flowers for the first time, showing powers of luminosity. This Dark Shard City of darkness now had hope, to bring the city into the light.

The magicians did not fail in their hard toil, as they brought forth a creation of light unknown. These magicians created a vine which spread out to the highest peak, wrapping its waxy leaves around every tower, casement and entranceway, all this magick idealism coming from a solitary bloom worn within the Princess's tresses.

It went from a simple vine to a web of art, thousands of trailing runners, repelling insects and birds. Under the moonlight they became a symphony, as the moon touched each flower, opening each under its spell-tide. All nightlong was the show of the petals, as they would turn in the wind, showing a different color, from the darkest blue to the whitest of whites, these blooms of magick staying mostly white under the solstice moon, and tightly closed by day. Opening only fully with the dusk to reveal not only their beauty, but the beauty of the dark city, eerie blue light of movement that came from inside, showing life dwelled and rested well within those walls of darkness.

The dark city was now a city of multihued illumination. Every crevice peeked of an eerie sapphire light making the city look surreal, this was the King's goal. Seeing this blue beacon of light, a weary traveler could not help but be drawn in, seeking company and a bed for the night. For one reason or another the Fallen Elves thought, in this manner, the 'others' would redeem them of their past unlawful codes and take them back into their society; but it was not to be.

Accepting their fate, they continued to live within the city of darkness blessed by its beauty and cursed by its elders, never to see their families again. They stayed in their Dark City of astounding plants which rivaled the moon itself. They were of the dark fairy folk, but still, feeling cast out from the others, they continued to build their city with ornate and elegance of pride. Magick crafters carved many things of dark ebony, obsidian and many dark and strange objects. Even though the city itself was dark, the dark elves were friendly.

Odysseus's mentor and teacher, Delmar, took over his entire studies and took him under his wing. Although Belisma was also a grand student; Delmar noticed Belisma took short cuts to get what he wanted, but was quick of wit. Delmar could not help but like his two prize students, choosing them both to study this flower called 'The Moon Glow'.

"You see, Odysseus, this flower has become so important to our King we must preserve its value, not only for the King, but also for our pretty little princess Daphne as well. I see the way you look upon her, trust me, it is better to study her flower than her being. I think she was born around the same time as you and I see the longing in both your eyes. I knew her mother well; it was a great loss to the King to lose her at his daughter's birth. I think, however, this is the reason he dotes on her so, for she looks so much like her mother. Now, let us be back to work, shall we?" Odysseus nodded and worked hard with Belisma, but his mind was still on the pretty Princess Daphne and her beauty. 'How could a simple student of wizardry win a princess's heart?'

Both Belisma and Odysseus were amazed at finding the many uses and strange ways of this delicate plant. They both watched in awe one night as Daphne and the magicians picked this flower and it immediately became like the shard it grew upon, therefore, pollinating was a careful process. The seeds extracted at dusk as soon as the flower opened and then planted into magickal terrain. Belisma and Odysseus worked in the labs for many hours. For instance, the flower, when crushed, turned to a sparkling blue/black powder. Mixing this powder with a small piece of the shard made a phenomenal piece of clothing in which one could actually move through and within the hard shards themselves. Both decided this information was too volatile to leak out to the general public without the permission of the King and Princess, as well as, the rest of their findings. Even the King agreed Delmar's Master Racknar should not know this particular information. Racknar, the Master School Teacher, seemed to frighten Daphne. And so, they all agreed this information would be known to the community. Nevertheless, as for the rest of their theories and observations, they felt all was well to tell the others.

Odysseus remembered well the discovery of the leaves, for example, when the glossy leaves, mixed with other special herbs of different colors, as a dye for instance, it became apparent students would then be able to use the wet paste for tapestries and paints. These paints could be mixed from a dull color to a high sheen, giving the user the ability for empathy, but only those who studied hard could master the mixtures of dyes and true colors of the spectrum to become a true seer.

They found the stems were woody enough to carve the delicate windpipes; many studied to become master woodworkers and could proclaim their art in other Kingdoms as trade. They could obtain this skill by vigilantly carving, drilling the precise holes, which took many a measurement, then turn them over to the enchanters for the final touch. These windpipes could then enchant, after many hours of practice, almost any animal. Students of taming usually started with the less significant of the species, such as a small pest, then to a larger living thing; learning to lure and enchant almost any beast. To tame a beast was only part of their lessons, another was to learn its lore, like the food it preferred the most, and how often it needed to eat, and so on.

They found the stamens of this flower were a powerful ingredient in controlling one's mind through dream spells.

This, too, was a very alluring prospect for many wizards and Sorceress, as a dream could linger on and on, like a song not easily shaken from mind.

Odysseus remembered the many black butterflies the flower attracted. They would cling to every vine during spring mating season, this itself was an amazing thing to observe. They came every year in swarms, as a beautiful blanket of wings to cover the city. These butterflies became the attraction of the year, flowing through the air and starting the season of Mayday. Again, this was long ago, inside the Dark Shard City.

Racknar, however, became curious of Belisma and Odyeuss's late night learning sessions and begun to question these two students, with no success and them being tight lipped. He then went directly to the King, who told him only what he already knew, making him even more suspicious of the 'why?' of these late night private sessions. Racknar straightened himself with chin up, as thoughts ran though his head. 'I am the master teacher here, why should I, of all people, be kept in the dark? I am more powerful than most of those pitiful magicians the King has hanging on his every word, why am I not trusted?'

True, Racknar was one of the most powerful of the city, teaching the dark arts and, for that reason, he was not trusted. It was, therefore, too easy to turn him towards the dark side, and with good reason; Racknar's mind was revolving that way. Racknar started his plans in motion, with a small band of mutinous friends, to turn the city against and overthrow the King. However, the majority of the city decided to remain good-willed and stay away from Racknar, which only made him more furious. He stood back and watched the good people of this large city bow to their good willed King and his rules. Racknar immediately backed away from this bad situation to make better plans. He needed more time.

Racknar then pledged himself to the King, as a good professor of wizardry, to help with the finalizing of the tunnel system running under the city, with the King's gratitude. The King knew he needed another powerful force in which to give his drawn-out plan of a system more motivation. Now, the tunnel system should go quick and efficiently. There is the time Racknar needed to plan and scheme, except for those pests; Belisma and Odysseus. So, he decided to send Delmar and his prized students on a quest to the 'Great Hall of the Magi'.

Odysseus and Belisma are thrilled to learn more, packing immediately to leave and, with them gone for a year or more, would give Racknar the time he needed to study Delmar's books and research. It took some time, for Delmar was tricky in hiding all his notes, as well as those of his students. But, after many attempts, he did finally find everything needed before they returned.

The Dark Shard City was now complete from top to bottom including a maze of underground tunnels, and of course, Racknar knew them all, the weaknesses and secret passages. Racknar was now a powerful wizard to reckon with, but he too had a weakness and that was Daphne. He even asked for her hand, but she recoiled, which made him furious!

Odysseus remembered when Racknar left the city, having issues with the King before he left. But, there were many things that Odysseus did not know about Racknar. Soon after his return, Delmar too disappeared, leaving Odysseus heartbroken with disbelief that his friend and mentor would suddenly pick up and merge into the night, without so much as a note of farewell. Odysseus and Belisma, after this incident, were soon placed in a high position that was uncommon for new graduates.

Years had passed since he had left to meet with the first King of the Mist, where Odysseus was now commissioned to protect and serve as wizard to the royal family. It was troubled times as the Cel'eset were striving to survive and was in need of an alliance with the middle North for protection and the North was in need of Magick.

Heated meetings and promises made between the Cel'eset's and the North Mist, only to the outcome of an arranged marriage between the first-born Princess of their new King of the Cel'eset and Prince of the Mist Place as a pledge of their alliance. Together, these two countries made a large stand against any worthy rival, plus a wealthy alliance. Odysseus had come to this palace and met for the first time, Mary Elizabeth.

With magickal powers she tried so hard to restrain, Odysseus was a wizard she could talk to and help through her troubled times. She was so young and beautiful to be wed off as a pawn, but then again, that was none of his doing.

Odysseus saw her through her wedding and could tell all was well between the mortal and the Cel'eset; she was happy with her new husband, and two friends, that of Piper Elf and himself to get through some terrible times.

Her first born passed every test and seemed normal in every way. Alexander, however, was having great issues with hidden powers, thinking himself evil. Only by rage of warrior fighting could he defeat almost anything and, once calmed, heal himself. Neither the Queen nor the wizard noticed his strange rage problems or his easy healing; only that Alex seemed to prefer his time alone.

Mary was so relieved when Victoria was born, thinking she too had her father's blood running through her veins, until one fateful day when Mary held her daughter up to the mirror on her first birthday before bed and saw Victoria was the image of Mary. Mary stood for a long while pondering in shock of her and her daughters eyes, which now glowed back at them in their reflection. Mary was beside herself and planned with the wizard on a special room for protection. Mary told him of her letters of an admirer, but she would not reveal to him his identity, therefore the wizard had no idea what they were up against or what possible threat this meant to the royal family.

And so it came to pass this secret room was built with magick for the child Victoria to hide within and be safe. The only ones who knew this was the Queen, King, the child, the now wizard and an Elvin boy, a painter of empathy, who came with the Queen from the swamp area as a so-called messenger between the two palaces. This small elfin boy, Piper Elf, has already painted a portrait of the Queen and at nightfall her sight came alive within the canvas, with glowing eyes.

The younger of these two children was showing remarkable panther like abilities. Odysseus would notice her light of feet and ability to fight, that he felt must be contained or all her secrets could be revealed and frighten the commoners. The perfect place for hiding her talents was her secret room. There was the child, Victoria. Even at an early age she began hiding disguise's and rough weapons. Odysseus kept an amusing eye on her; yes, he would like to see her grow with all her Mother's abilities.

Mary had made him feel he could take on the world then, his first crush, he smiled to himself. She was one of 'The People of the Light'. She was a Cel'eset, where he was one of the Dark Shard, the fallen, coming from the same race, but brought up in two different cities'. Maybe this was why she did not tell him everything. He had never told her where he originated, she seemed to 'just know about people'. He promised to keep her children and their children safe.

This promise was why he had to find out what was happening at the city. He was feeling darkness in his heart, as if it no longer existed, at least not to the eye. He was panicking. His heart raced home only to see nothing, gone, all gone, as if it had just vanished from the world and thousands of voices cried out in hopelessness.

He knew then he must go questing to the shrines of magick, shrines he had only been to once, as a boy, with Belisma. Each shrine was hard to find and once there he has to pass them. It was the only way to learn how to fight the thoughts, growing evil thoughts, now entering into and taking over his mind.

CHAPTER 4

Out of the Darkness
and into the Present

Myst, sensing the darkness enveloping Odysseus' mind, quickly looked at his hand. His ring was glowing in its intensity. Without thought or consequence she quickly slid the offensive ring from his finger. After removing the ring she could feel the power within and immediately regretted her impulsive action. At once he was wide-awake and alert, grasping her wrist, which made her cry out in pain and shock. Odysseus looked upon her in an almost loathing way as he continued to tighten his grip on her wrist.

"How did you manage to remove my ring?" Odysseus questioned quite loud and possessively, oblivious of what was going on around him.

"I took it off when I saw you were in distress. Here, it is yours." Myst, taken back by his shouting, seeing the wild look in his eyes, quickly opened her hand and held it out for him.

Odysseus snatched it out of her grasp as he released her wrist. Myst rubbed at her wrenched wrist.

"What is wrong with you? I am not a common thief."

Odysseus observed his still attached finger, wiggling it, wondering how Myst had removed it without removing the finger itself. Only high wizards of his choosing could remove this ring, or he could remove it freely of his own will, without the loss of the digit, as did Delmar (his previous master). He saw Myst looking at him in wonder and somewhat hurtful feelings, but Odysseus did not perceive her inquisitiveness, focused only on placing the now offensive article suspiciously back in his pouch.

Myst wondered at his rings source and why. "If it were truly his, why he would keep it hidden? If it were indeed his possession, why not wear it all the time or secret it from his friends?"

Finally, seeing the questioning look upon Myst's face, Odysseus hastily apologized for his coarse treatment and pleaded her forgiveness. He saw the raised eyebrow, the questioning look on her face. She would never be satisfied until she knew everything. Leaning into her, as if in a moment of weakness, he whispered, "On my given word, I will tell you all you need to know of this covert, but later. For now this should be our little secret." His eyes pleaded to keep this episode between them.

Myst nodded in agreement. "But, you will tell me about this ring later, all and in its entirety my friend, because bruises are hard to explain, even harder to understand by your intended. I shall hold you to a great reminder of many promises." She smiled at Odysseus.

"So, it comes down to a sorcerers mark, does it? Alright, my clever apprentice, I swear on my ancestors you shall know the whole story, but later." They quietly gathered their wits about them and tried to stand, without much success.

Myst finished their strange banter before anyone noticed by directing Odysseus's awareness to the others. "The spell is now complete. Look, even Sarpeden is having trouble lifting her wing to free our new Lotus. This spell took its toll on us all, especially you, Odysseus." She pointed throughout the cavern for him to see each of his participants in shock and trepidation of what they may have just lost to create a being that could destroy them all. As she watched him take in the sight of his family, friends and those he had come to love lying about on the cavern floor, he had a troublesome thought of what he had done.

However, it was Sarpeden who looked upon him in a knowing gaze. He could swear her heavy eyelid gave him a blink of knowledge. 'Did she give him the dream of his boyhood and other knowledge? Did she know everything of the Cel'eset's or of other dragons perhaps and, for that matter, did she put the knowledge into his mind and know what his ring actually meant or . . . ?' No time to ponder on it. Sarpeden finally managed to raise her weary wing high enough to allow all to see a dazed and confused Lotus, as she stumbled out from under Sarpenden's wing.

Odysseus and Myst gazed upon their new creation with tired eyes, as did all the rest. The whole group sat in awe, watching this woman as she emerged from beneath the wing. They waited in anticipation to see if this was the same Lotus they sent under the wings of a magickal dragon. Was this still Myst's dusty, hard working, meek and timid Lotus, or a flame of evil, in which they were too weak to fight. She could take them all now, with a sweep of an angry hand, for what they had just done to her and all would be lost.

Lotus came stumbling to them. "Where am I?" She spun on Sarpeden, pointing an accusing finger. "And you! What goes here that you would be in this condition?" She looked around in concern, "Were we attacked down here? How did I get down here?" Lotus ranted on and on with simple questions, looking from one person to another for answers, getting only silence. She shook her head trying to remember what had transpired, before she lost consciousness, "I feel strange." Lotus finished and sat on a nearby piece of boulder, she held her head.

Odysseus affirmed with a smile then a frown, as he proclaimed, "We have now created a new color of magick. A shimmering fire, gold and unpredictable in the future generations, as a magickal person of unknown heritage. A blend of a fire breathing golden dragon, a fosterling at that, and the combination of all our talents."

"What are you speaking of, this magick mutual act of the elements, Wizard Odysseus? What really happened here?" Lotus was total in a stupor of mystification. "I had the strangest dream of floating in a golden cloud and there was a moment when I felt pure rage inside this cloud, then there were painful memories replaced by happiness and love. Can you explain these strange things that are happening to me, please?"

Ignoring Lotus's last announcement, Odysseus turned to Myst. "This should be an interesting subject to study," he whispered with a shrug. "Shall we all check to see if we have our magick powers back?" Odysseus looked towards Lotus. We will explain all, once we are safely in the towers above." The rest managed to make a successful attempt, allowing them to simple magick. "Seems our powers will be restored wholly with some respite. Our magick shall come back quickly then." They sighed in relief.

Odysseus's gaze settled on his small daughter and Sarpeden. Seeing them together, not only in friendship, in complete comfort, but there was more . . . what seemed to be a bonding. He was in great hope the drain of this magick did not damage the dragon permanently. He had very little knowledge of dragons at this time and, considering the connection between Willow and Sarpeden, he decided Willow should remain there with the dragon for a long rest. Sarpeden was delighted for the companionship and assured Odysseus she would be in excellent hands. Willow gave him a hug and told her father she would be sure the dragon was well fed. His daughter, Willow, was now caring for this large dragon; her new friend.

A now weary Myst hugged Willow, placing a finger upon her nose and said, "I knew there was something special about you, but could not put my finger on it."

"Odysseus said to be careful and not to tell you why I was here. So, I met you, a great sorceress, and had my fun with others," Willow replied with a smile, thinking of Amber.

Thanking Sarpeden for her magick, except for Lotus who did not notice any and was trying to figure out how she even got down there. She was still in complete and utter confusion.

Lotus felt strange, as if she were still in a golden dream, and trying to pull herself together, she was thinking aloud. "Let's see, I was upstairs trying to listen to some kind of plan. Then, I can slightly remember a small boy, who kept jumping up and down, making faces, or was that a dream?" In any event, as she turned on the group, "how is it I came to be down here in the caverns and why? What are you all up to, as I sense a change in the wind? I feel quite unusual and require knowing what happened here."

Odysseus quickly piped up with a simple solution. "We all held hands and combined our magick so you could levitate, then you fainted, just as we reached the bottom. Can you not remember now, my dear Lotus? I suggest we try the up part, without the fainting if you please, for I am in no condition at this time to be carrying you anymore." Odysseus looked to her with raised eyebrow, then to Myst. It was a splendid suggestion to see if the magick in reality was successful an experimentation to see if Lotus had more control over her powers.

They all required her force of power and her inner strength within the circle to ascend. "For now, my dear Lotus, would you mind helping an old man off the floor? I feel quite faint myself and we shall either ascend or amble up all these stairs, it's up to you," Odysseus lied. Odysseus held out the hand and watched Lotus cross the room to help him. He quickly replaced the ring.

However, before she reached her hand out to him, she looked at him with much curiosity, "Odysseus, what happened to your hair and beard, are you alright?"

"Oh, 'tis nothing to worry about my dear, once you have a chance to get to know me a little better, you will know something's go awry from time to time." He continued to wave his hand upward, motioning for her to come closer. After a moment of hesitation, she decided all must be well—why would Odysseus lie to her. Giving him a hand up, they both abruptly felt a warm jolt go through their bodies.

"What was that" asked Lotus, rubbing her tingling hand?

"It was nothing, my dear," shrugging off the shock transferred between them, his whole body felt a bit more regenerated and warmer in the chilliness of the cave. Odysseus realized this ring had the power to pass some of her energy back to him.

Delmar, wore this ring at all times and that is why his Master never touched his students. He must have known this ring could transfer his students' powers to himself and, if not controlled appropriately, it could drain them of all powers. He knew also knew he was slipping away and could no longer protect it, so he gave the ring to the one student who he trusted to protect it. This was the same ring which drained Alex's mother. Was there more than one ring? Did Belisma ever find this elusive ring? He doubted there were two of the same, but possible, if Belisma was within a secret faction of evil wizards. This would mean all members of the guild would have a similar ring if not the same.

Odysseus pointed to Lotus and asked her to lead the way to the dark turret. He whispered to Myst, "Do you observe new confidence in the way she holds herself? Her head held high, as she is almost gliding? We have changed this person and we must watch her closely for a time-agreed?" Myst nodded her accord.

Lotus, turned towards the winds that lifted her golden fine hair. Raising her hands against the battering winds, as if but a minor pest which buzzed around her face, the winds unexpectedly came to a silent calm. The look of astonishment flitted across her delicate face as she turned to the with wide eyes and asked, "How did I do that?" Truly amazed at her sudden ability to control the winds without thinking, Lotus looked at her hand and wrist, noticing for the first time the golden glint to her skin. "How did I get this amazing color to my skin, and how did I, without contemplation or reason, just happen to know how to calm the winds?" She stood totally baffled, still disoriented.

Immediately, to take Lotus's mind off the goings on of what had just happened, Odysseus nodded and with a gesture of his finger made a circle in mid-air. Myst joined hands with Odysseus, waiting patiently for Lotus to unite the circle. "Now let us concentrate and see if you have learned your lesson of levitation. Concentrate and take us slowly and easily in an upward manner, if you please, my dear Lotus," she joined them completing the circle.

Odysseus's sigh of relief could be heard as it echoed off the tower walls. They felt the liberation as all of their feet gradually left the ground. Odysseus waited on Lotus's lead, as he and Myst were well drained of their power, and was relying on Lotus to lift them all to the balcony. 'Yes, she would become stronger and even might become a new generation.'

Lotus's glee at her ability to levitate showed in her face and congratulations abound from Odysseus and Myst. Then there was another face, a not so gleeful face. It was the face of Spyder, with a challenging and sudden outburst, wanting to know what happened to Lotus and Willow.

"What do you mean, what happened to me?" asked Lotus, as she also noticed the impressed looks of Vickie, Nate and Alex. While Spyder looked angry, the rest looked mystified.

"This," Myst said, as she slid out the full mirror. It was now or never. Lotus should know what they had done and why.

'This cannot be,' thought Lotus, as she turned about. Odysseus saw the astonishment in her eyes. As Odysseus tried to enlighten her on what they had done, only a small amount of words filtered into her reasoning process, as she gazed at herself in the reflection. What she saw was a gold dress clinging intimately to her body, covered partially by a thin, pale hooded cloak, the color of an ashen mist that filtered through the trees, yet showed you nothing. Her hair was now long, out of the pins that always held it off the back of her neck. Clean as with the shining of the sun. She had the same gold bands on her small wrists, a thick band collar, and a small-jeweled headdress, just as Myst! However, Myst was a Sorceress. Lotus looked down to see a fine braided cord hanging low upon her hips. She now was armed with a dagger of gold, gems embedded in its handle.

"This, my dear, is for you to present to Aries as a bridal gift with all your love and allegiance," Odysseus stated. He had poured some kind of obnoxious smelling potion into a vial, spilling over his hand. He crossed the small space, to run this hand through her hair, pretending to admire her.

"What is that foul odor?" Lotus asked, backing away, as Odysseus placed the remembrance potion on her.

"What odor?" Odysseus looked most offended. Lotus had to admit she smelled it no more, as if it vaporized. He hoped Aries remembered her as his childhood love, and that this brew would lend a hand.

Lotus was mesmerized as she reached up to touch the gold metal piece around her neck that claimed her Sorceress and then it struck her like a rock as she turned from the mirror. "This spell of charm and enchantment will not last, Aries will be furious with us all. You cannot be serious; you plan to leave me before this sorcery of glamour wears off. Oh, I cannot do this!" Plus, she had been a mage of Belisma, there was no denying this and, in her own mind, knew her instruction in evil made everything impractical for Aries.

Odysseus saw doubt in her eyes and before she could consider the outcome he started his words of hopeful romance, knowing this was her weakest spot. "Not anymore you aren't," said Odysseus with a smile. "You have the power of a wizard, a sorceress, a special dragon, a magickal child and this, my dear, is permanent, not a glamour spell. This is our bequest to you."

Lotus turned away, with the whisper, "He shall kill us all when he knows who I am. Even I know there are no short cuts in making me more powerful."

"Well, my tender apprentice, with all of us gathered together using our but meager magick and with this special dagger, we have made you very special indeed. Please do not loathe us." Myst pressed a special dragger in her hand.

"Willow, where is she," demanded a red-faced Spyder, hopping now as if a toad on a hot flat rock?

"Oh, Spyder, she is just spending some time with our new pet and feeding her. She knows how to get up and down from there and get Sarpeden out if necessary. Don't worry.

"At least I won't be making her a snack like that ole draggie might," he grumbled, starting once more to worry and pace.

Lotus pleaded; "I still don't know how this is going to work."

"Let us do the talking when we get there," said Odysseus, "and all will be well." Odysseus saw she may be powerful, but still the timid woman. The spell worked, letting this delicate flower contain its beauty and love for peace. Myst sent a servant boy with a message that she would like a private audience with Aries. Also, for the boy to tell Aries she had friends accompanying her, three in all, as the rest of the group must wait for them in the tower. Myst saw Odysseus take this time for a rest and to gather his thoughts of the impeding meeting with this hotheaded King, Aries. She could see in his eyes he was, for some reason, dreading the inevitable event to come.

"Who is this pesky boy you felt you had to bring with you?" Myst asked of Odysseus. She was to wearisome to handle this situation. Her powers were regaining once again, but slowly, she was in need of rest and this 'Spyder' was absolutely distracting. She found him into everything, snooping, spying, touching things he knew nothing of and just a plain pest.

"This, my dear, is our thief, lock pick and all around jester to keep up our spirits," Odysseus explained with a knowing smile, as he pushed the unaware boy toward this powerful woman.

"Meet Spyder a special friend of Alex."

"Well, Spyder," making him scatter back up behind Odysseus, "if you are a friend in this group, then you have my protection as well." Myst giggled.

Spyder noticed smoke trailing up and around her fingers. "At your service, Milady." Myst did notice the quick inspection of her hand, as to where the energy ball had come from and where it had gone. Odysseus was correct, he was amusing. She could not help but smile down upon this boy.

Nathaniel poked Alex in the ribs and chuckled, "Now you know how it feels. Seems you are going to have the same problem I do with my Vickie. Are you the jealous type?" They both laughed a tense laugh. They had all noticed the drain on the faces of Odysseus and Myst when they returned. Wondering, but afraid to ask what had happened down there in the dark.

Alex was worried for Myst; she needed her pond of mist to heal her and he saw it in her eyes. She was just plain homesick. The sooner they were home the better off they all shall be.

It was not long before the messenger boy returned with the reply. "Aries will see you now, Milady Myst, and your escort." The boy never looked into the tower, past the door; he had heard rumors of 'things' happening in the west tower. Standing straight, the boy did only as was told, nothing more, nothing less, as he quickly turned and led the strange looking party to Aries chambers.

Odysseus had time enough to cover a very nervous Lotus in her golden cape, including the low hung hood, covering her face, resting on her shoulders. The others left to entertain themselves, leaving them to wait. Telling them not to worry. Alex drank more brandy as he paced, Nathaniel watched Vickie and Spyder having a grand time waiting as Spyder snooped and Vickie trying to keep him out of trouble.

It was as if they were all on some vacation, playing the snoops and acting like children, until Spyder came upon a very deep wide well, hidden under a platform. So, that is how wizards get there water! They both smiled, thinking the same thoughts, a bath! Spyder brought up water using ropes and pulleys tucked in the low rafters after several draws. Water heating on the fire. Nathaniel found the bath behind a very large partition. They flew into action, trying to keep their minds off the wait of finally being clean after their ordeal in the caverns below, making as little noise as possible.

They found some weapons and some cloths to clean with. Hopefully, when the wizards returned, all would be well and they might as well take their minds off their worries, by staying busy.

As the bath was drawn, Alex piped up. "Might as well have a bath while we wait. Ladies first," Alex gestured to Vickie. "And if all fails, at least we fight, and may die, clean."

"You just had to add that last bit of dismay, didn't you, my brother?" Vickie grabbed a cloth, twirled it from-end-to-end and snapped him in the chest, as she walked behind the screen. Vickie could not help but smile at seeing her big, strong brother grab at his chest in pain at the small cloth's snap.

CHAPTER 5

The Walk Towards Aries

Myst, Odysseus, and a reluctant Lotus followed the boy out of the comfortable mages tower. Odysseus, expecting an open connection as between most towers, was pleasantly surprised when they stepped onto an enclosed domed passageway instead of a customary walk way. He was amazed at these well-placed lead glass windows, which only faced the courtyard below. The other side only showed metal cover slits, made for the archers to release in case of assault; it was there that a few well placed guards stood. All the way though this covered tunnel. Plenty of warm glowing lanterns designed as comfort for traveling between the two buildings.

Myst listened as Odysseus's mind jumped completely off track from one subject to another. She could see that he, as a wizard, was enthralled in taking notes for his own improvements to the Mist Palace. With a knowing smile Myst prodded him to move on, remembering the first time she had walked through this lit tunnel, so high off the ground and thinking of Alex, knowing of his affection for heights.

It also seemed Odysseus was not fond of this loftiness, as he followed swiftly alongside Myst.

Heavy wooden doors blocked their entrance to Aries private domain. The small boy pulled out a ring of keys, inserting one into the elaborate latch. The latch made no sound as he turned the key; when the latch unfastened the boy swung open the weighty doors as if they were but tapestry hanging on a wall. He then turned to bow to his Sorceress in dismissal. "Milord awaits you, Milady, you know the way?" The boy nodded, as not in question.

"I thank you, Winsor. Yes, I will lead the party the rest of the distance." Myst led, past the boy, down the wide steps. The steps spread out into the wide rooms of Aries chambers. Small arches, which supported the small tunnel, could not compare to those of the massive ones of the palace, as the group spilled out onto the fifth floor.

They now stood in the domain of all beauty. Aries' father, Alyas, had built this large and impressive fifth floor with three entrances into this suite and one hidden escape. He had thought of everything to protect his wife and children for their safety. Only he and his wife knew the location of the secret escape and it was only to be used in times of anticipated war. Aries did not know about the caves under the tower and his father died before he could pass on much of his secrets. Aries deemed the tower safe.

Here stood the shrine of Alyas' now dead, wife. Myst dragged her feet, for within this area held a showcase of many exquisite things. The case itself sat upon a large teakwood table. The elaborately designed table with carved legs: each leg telling a story in a different language, punctuations made in tiny gems. Each wide leg stood on a great-clawed foot, which grasped a crystal ball of transparency. Inside held showing off each priceless item in a lining of garnet velvet.

In the center of this great memorial held a priceless ring; it was the wedding ring of Aries' stepmother, a spectacular array of garnets and emeralds. This ring was made for a small hand in the shape of a delicate rose, which brought a large garden to life. Ariel's journals open to be seen to show worn pages bestowing stunning pressed flowers. Her diary contained all secrets of her planting, pollinating and the origins of the flowers.

Myst looked to Odysseus with the knowing look. Ariel was more than just a beautiful woman, perhaps her journal was more than what it seemed. Mayhap, she was not only a healer with her potions, oils and things, but for magickal purposes. Myst pointed to one particular entry, which seemed to be more of a chant. She looked to Odysseus, "Were her talents hidden in sonnets and poems in which she would read to these people so not to scare them?

"All these poems Ariel wrote are now faded, but I have used the copy spell as best I could," Odysseus replied. "We can study them at a later time."

Myst looked to Odysseus. In a whisper she continued while the rest admired this elegant case. "It is my belief Ariel, by some means; cast a code, or charms of kind, to shelter her people and her personal effects from Belisma. I get the instinct impression she not only feared this wizard, but in her passing away, she was also trying to tell someone a dark secret. See, here are letters to Queen Ariel from those whom loved her and, as you can see, these too rhyme in the same form of verse. It is as if they all feared something or someone and felt it essential to communicate in secret system. This is a very impressive showcase of affection and magick. The big question here for me was who cast the spell to shield all her things? Aries too was amazed when I could translate most of the writing and unlock this cabinet."

Odysseus stroked his beard and in simple words replied, "So am I my dear Myst, for I found you a simple peasant girl, existing in the woodland among the foliage and the animals and now . . . well, I just do not know what to make of you. No one really understood why there were pebbles of faded rose quartz amongst the flowers, spilling out of a garnet bag, haphazardly tied with a frayed golden drawstring.

However, it was this castle which drew Myst's attention the most. The drawbridge was made of gold, a delicate piece. Myst pondered on this particular piece, as the stones grew more faded each time she looked upon it. The rose color slowly drained out, like sand running out of an hourglass. There stood a riddle on the castle, simply saying;

> Castle of love, which stands so tall,
> With a love that shall withstand all,
> But if love is lost it turns to sand,
> The castle shall fall within your hands.

There were rumors about this garden of hers. Supposedly, Alyas closed it soon after her death, not being able to bear looking upon it again and yet it holds another riddle on heavy iron gates placed somewhere within these garden walls. Neither the peasants nor the servants were permitted into her garden, neither to visit nor tend to it. I am afraid that by now 'tis quite overgrown and well veiled after all this time." Myst never looked upon this illusive floral garden. Actually, she was never really interested in looking for it, as she thought it would only be another dismal distraction.

Myst continued the story. "Alyas could not bear to see this garden after his wife's death. Locking the gates and simply walking away. "Odysseus, this castle reeks of secrets, lies and riddles. I cannot tolerate it much longer. I grow weary of this tryst." Myst's mind then suddenly filled with doubts and apprehensions about what they were about to do. Would the peasants take to Lotus or would they would never forget their Queen and her beautiful garden, this garden made from her love; the one thing Myst could never fix in this Kingdom. Myst glanced back at Lotus, perhaps, just perhaps, this little Lotus could. This was their new hope for themselves and for this Kingdoms survival. Lotus would have a large burden to bear, not only for a King that reined upon all they could see, but his people as well.

Myst squared her shoulders, shook off these troubled feelings, and took a deep breath. The doors at once opened for them into an abyss of shadows.

Aries always kept it dark; much like his disposition and Myst knew this to be unhealthy. Maybe his Lotus could bring him into the light once more. As Myst passed the guards, she noticed they wore soft enhanced leather and lighter magickal armor of her design. She was weary and allowed her mind to again wander back to several days past.

She and the blacksmith had worked closely together to devise pieces of armor. Being lighter and cooler in the west just simply made more sense and it made the heavy chain mail and breast-plates obsolete. Metal and magick combined worked very well, but Aries resisted the first test, fearing death would result to one of his guards. Myst tried to reassure the King it had been verified on a stuffed dummy. The other guards even stood back with distrust when the experiment was complete. None of the guards would even try a piece on, although it was a temptation. Finally, one valiant soul stood out amongst the rest and volunteered for the testing.

"You just can't have your men dropping in this heat," Myst pleaded to Aries, when the first Amour came out. Just test it," she said, and tried to hand him a sword.

"I will not shed the blood of my own people!" Aries barked at her, crossing his arms in refusal.

"Very well, I always wanted to do this, especially lately," she shot back. With eyes flashing at him she grasped the sword with all her might and lunged at the chest of the unprepared guard wearing the new amour. The guard stared at the new Sorceress in shock for a split second before he stumbled back and fell.

Everyone gasped, thinking she had certainly killed him in anger. Myst simply caught him off guard, and no one seemed more shaken than the knight did. He brushed himself off and looked for a wound not there. He stood slowly, looking at the broken half of the sword that lay beside him. He then looked up into a shadowed woman, hands on her hips, the other half of the sword still in her hand. Astounded, he still checked for a wound, then announced, "It works, although it did sting a bit, Milady." He bowed before her with a smile, kissed her hand and then turned to show a slight scratch upon the armor. He removed the breastplate and held it out for the people to see for themselves how light the amour was and to show not a single muscle, not a single scratch upon his body, although he thought there might be a slight bruise from her strike; she was quite strong for a little woman. The men all surrounded the blacksmith, questions flying to its making, avoiding Myst altogether.

Myst stomped back towards her tower, swinging the now broken sword back and forth, feeling reasonably unappreciated. On the way, Myst passed Aries. She stopped long enough to press the sword with force into Aries chest, eyes still flashing in fury. She remembered Aries looking down at this broken sword, as he reached up to grasp it from her hand, now pressed forcefully into his chest. He then looked into her eyes with disbelief and contained humor as he watched her saunter away from him without looking back. Still in anger, she heard the shout from him, "Well, I guess it does work."

She turned, seeing the almost amused look, the slight smile on his face. She smiled back; thinking this was as close as they had been to an understanding. He now knew she would protect the palace and maybe, just maybe, they had the beginning of a friendship connecting them.

Myst heard the harsh clearing of Odysseus's throat. She was back to matters at hand, peering into the dark chambers, looking for Aries, turning to Odysseus she saw in his eyes the awe for Aries rooms.

Myst and Lotus, having been in these rooms many times before, thought nothing of it, but this happened to be Odysseus's first time.

Myst always wondered if Ariel were such a generous and beautiful woman, did the father of Aries build this chamber just for her. And, if built in her honor, why was the young King lured away to have a bastard child by a peasant woman or even by a concubine? In fact, if true, why would the Queen herself give this woman coin to protect the boy from this wizard and an amulet to prove his heritage? Ariel was so in love as the tales were told, it made no sense; another riddle.

Odysseus did not know where to look first; his eyes adjusting to the low lighting. There were high smooth ceilings, painted carefully of women playing with children, many pink wild roses without thorns and more. On the walls hung paintings of maidens and fine gentlemen walking by a waterfall fed by the sea. The stepmother of Aries had a touch of flair in watercolor. All these paintings bore her signature.

A great fireplace beheld polished stonework. A wide mantle, which displayed a combination of shared exquisiteness. A collection of handsome swords, daggers and manly beauty, as well as the beauty of tall imported perfumed bottles. Tanned fur rugs were the display on the polished stone floor, which were surrounded by imported tossed satin and velvet tasseled pillows. Alabaster statues, from all over their world, brought in and placed carefully on wide pedestals of marble. Alyas was unquestionably a collector; probably taken from faraway lands or purchased from other artisans from other Kingdoms.

Moonstone alabaster was rare to find enough to make this many statues, unbelievable. Statues of men and woman stood strategically around the showpiece of this magnificent room and one of the most focal points of the room. The bath or sunken pool was placed in the very center of this enormous room, filled with clear blue water, smooth as glass. This chamber was built for love, but it was love Myst could never feel for Aries.

Myst led Odysseus and Lotus to a large stone table. The carved wooden chairs were plump, upholstered in light colored satin and tassels.

CHAPTER 6

A New Beginning for Aries

Set upon a grand table, candles held in brass and crystal holders cast eerie lights all about which made the room fill the room with a ghostly light. Platters held exotic fruits and golden chalices filled with wine for their pleasure.

Aries joined them, a look of suspicion upon his face. Aries knew Odysseus and now approached the table curiously, disappointment clear on his face. "I see we are not here to make wedding plans, unless Odysseus is our new wedding planner." Aries definitely prepared for a long chat of colors, ceremony and party arrangements.

In his excitement at seeing Myst, Aries utterly forgot to dismiss Amber, his concubine. She stayed still and quiet, tucked in his bed, listening to every word. Amber as surprised as he, and even more delighted in thinking this clever sorceress thought of yet another way to escape the wedding. This would give her the time she needed to persuade Aries to love her only or at least give her the heir. Aries looked down upon Odysseus, Myst and this gold clad person with disdain.

"What is it you want from me now, wizard, and how did you get past my guards with a woman? You, without doubt, stand out in a crowd with your billowing robes of purple and flowing gold." Aries stared at Odysseus, as he kicked his chair around; the chair back came to rest at tables edge. He sat, set his arms on the back of the chair, resting his elbows on the table. His head came down to his hands, eyeing the trio that dare make another proposal. Tense feelings reached out through the air like static bolts, touching each person in a different way. After a long, silent, uncomfortable moment, Aries saved them all the trouble, starting the conversation to let them know he was not afraid and ready to fight to keep what they already gave him.

"Seems the north is not very good at keeping their word," he drummed out. "First I was promised a beautiful princess, and she was beautiful, unfortunately predisposed. Then, Myst, who promised me beauty and magick. With you at my side I have all I need. What more could you possibly offer me now?"

"So you may think, but do you really have all you want?" Odysseus interrupted this onslaught of insults.

Aries dropped his eyes to the table in defeat. In truth, the only one he ever wanted could not be there. These people would never know though; how could they? His Kingdom needed a wife, magick, and they shall have it! She was promised! It did bring back thoughts of a girl he once knew. She disappeared suddenly when he was a child. He looked up at the wizard once again, determination flared in his eyes. "I shall have what was promised," Aries demanded, pounding his fist on the table.

"You are happy with Myst, knowing she does not love you, Aries?" Odysseus was blunt. This caught Aries off guard.

"I was hoping she would come to love me in time. I am a lonely man without a mate, nor heir to share this palace with me." His tone was sad, even to his own ears, pathetic to Amber as she sat furious in hatred in his bed. 'Lonely,' she thought, 'without love?'

"Aries, make no mistake, for I have come to care for you. I truly do care, but my love will always belong to another. I thought loyalty and honor would be enough for you, but once I came here, I discovered it was not enough for either of us." Myst placed a hand over his, he looked up at her and saw the weary, sad girl he had made her. Myst spoke with stark truth to her words. Aries heard it plainly and Amber heard it in delightful song. The one thing Aries did admire about Myst, but she was right, he did not love her, and she could not love him. Myst smiled at him, a hopeful smile.

"I do, however, know a beautiful woman who does love you. She is talented in magick, and though untested, will have the strength and heart to protect your Kingdom." Myst thought to spill this out while Aries was vulnerable. Amber's glee now short lived; what was this witch up to now? She needed more time to be with his child, as she pressed her ear closer to the edge of the bed.

His eyes hardened. "And who, pray tell, is this wonderful woman?" Aries asked in a mocking tone, dropping Myst's hand. Folding his arms across his chest, tipping his chair, as if a small boy, he challenged gravitation.

"My apprentice, her name is Lotus. She is shy, but learning, learning fast, and Aries, she loves you." Myst waited his decision and without hesitation she got one.

"Aries gets another pawn? Hell, I cannot even see her face for that hood covering it!" Aries roared kicking the chair aside in frustration. He shoved against the table in his rage, strength enough to upset a pair of goblets, making everyone in the room jump. Even Amber jumped, almost falling from her perch on the side of his bed where she had been straining to hear every word; even she had never seen this flare of displeasure.

"No, 'tis true, I am not a pawn," the petite girl in gold protested, as a tiny hand slammed the dagger on the table with an unexpected pound. "This is my magickal gift to you, to protect you and this palace with my every breath and with all my love." Lotus was suddenly bold, her voice rose in anger, an anger even Aries heard. She feared she crossed the bounds, after all she'd given up for this man and was now losing him as he moved away. She reached out to stop him, her cape dropping to the floor as she grasped his sleeve. Myst and Odysseus were impressed with her new found boldness. Aries paused as he stared at Lotus' tiny hand on his arm, he turned to look into the clear blue eyes with a hint of gold.

A recognition, a flashback of the childhood girl he once knew, overwhelmed him. A scent of flowers came from her cape as it billowed to the floor. She once lived in the forest with her grandmother and made promises of marriage when they were older One day he went to see her and found the hut burned to the ground; they were all gone. He returned for her every day in suspense, that one day, she would return to him, but she'd disappeared from their village. This could not be her. Something stirred deep in his chest, a flutter of hope, perhaps? He still mourned her loss, knowing he would never love anyone but her again. He knew this was right. Aries finally found a maiden that looked more the part of his Queen and the people would love her without question. Knowing the peasants distrusted Myst, not only because of her foreign origins and dark hair, but for some reason there lay in their hearts malicious gossip and totally uncalled for deception. This maiden, this lady of blonde hair, blue eyed and fair of skin would surely win their hearts as she had his.

"This is your apprentice of magick?" he asked, shaking out of this spell.

"Lotus is ready to wed when you say," Odysseus announced. "No delays, and I agree to stay as long as it takes to make her a sorceress to protect you, your people and your palace. That is her promise to you, if you release Myst of her duties here." Odysseus pointed to the dagger on the table. Everyone looked to Odysseus, not knowing what to say, this was clearly not part of the plan.

Aries agreed to all terms immediately, without realizing, still stunned by the sight of this girl. He kept his questions to himself, for now; as Myst said, she was untested.

Amber started to dress, preparing to slip quietly out of the room. She yanked on her flimsy clothing, her mind racing, her anger too great. 'How dare they?' The look on Aries face told her enough and her still without child. Amber was running out of time and she knew it! "This will never do," she hissed to herself, as she eased from the room. How could Aries do this to her? She had been loyal to his every need at anytime of the day or the night. Easing his pathetic pain and listening to his wishful talk of a new Queen. How could those dimwit witches fail at such an easy task to stop those pathetic people? She grabbed her cloak. "I will fix this," she muttered under her breath, as she stomped in resolve to get her vengeance. Using the escape-way, she let the darkness embrace her as she headed toward the woodland.

"Those witches told me of their coming and they could stop them. I need more power. These potions are not working; I should be heavy with child now; those bumbling fools and their foolish attempts, the potion needs to be stronger!" Her mind was enraged. "I know who will help me for information, and I will be rewarded as Aries' wife!" Amber spat on her way through the dark forest. She needed a diversion, a delay to give her time. She needed a stronger potion to drug the King, stronger yet to carry an heir to the throne and be queen by next moon. "The witches owe me and they will pay!" Amber ranted all the way through the forest in search of her witches. They could show her the way to the sorcerer she sought or they will burn.

Myst dragged her heels to thank Aries, for he just made the best decision he would ever make. She reminded him gently that, with Odysseus here as well and his teachings, "If people hear great booms from the west tower, they should not worry, not all spells work the first time."

"Don't worry, Myst, this will not be the first wizard to keep me on my toes," Aries teased. His eyes shone with the easy light of friendship, not strained or tense, as with their engagement.

"The only differences between great booms from Belisma and those of Lotus, is now I will feel an impulse to run to see to her welfare," Aries replied.

Myst giggled at his sudden jollity. Aries kissed the back of her hand and, for the first time, the gesture did not seem forced or cold. "Good luck to you, lady Myst and how did Odysseus manage these castle walls without announcement? I take it I have more friends within my castle walls I should be aware of?"

"Yes, my liege," Myst replied, without giving information as to how many or where they might be. She only smiled in silence. Aries gave up, asking how many rooms should be prepared for the morrow. She was afraid to mention the Dragon below, not yet. As of now, Aries was a very happy man.

He went to bed, hardly noticing Amber was gone, but for her still lingering heavy perfume, an almost gagging scent compared to that which wafted from Lotus's cape of gold. Aries looked about with a scratch of his chin; he was thinking how people get in and out around him without his notice. He and Odysseus unquestionably must talk on plugging holes within his castle. He did not like people snooping around throughout the castle and it would be a very good way for an inside attack. He also noticed Amber being very amorous as of late, he must be very careful of his actions, of their outcome. He remembered how he felt when he found his father still lived and Aries swore not to have a bastard child. Amber was definitely rushing him. She made many a moment uncomfortable by grabbing and holding him tight. But there would be no bastard child from him, or a scandal for his new wife to deal with. There would be no more sleeping with Amber.

He gathered the servants, calling for fresh linens, lighter drapes, and a bath. In passing, he told the guards Amber was no longer allowed on this floor. He felt like a boy in love for the first time, all over again. He hardly slept that night waiting for morning to see this beauty again. The servants seemed to be just as excited as their new King as they arrived at his doors, bursting through the room and opening all his windows for the first time since harvest. Billowing soft white curtains pushed out the musty air and brought forth the new spring sun with a touch of violet fragrance on the breeze. Aries felt clean, fresh from the bath and late night of cleaning, wanting all to be perfect for his bride-to-be did not seem to slow him down.

He sent for his shy Lotus and did not have long to wait before she was announced for his audience. The messenger boy strolled into his chambers with a broad smile on his face. The boy turned to take his leave when Aries saw her there in all her beauty. Still donning her cloak of gold, she seemed to glide toward him as if in a dream. Reaching him, she curtsied low of body and head and in words soft, which wafted up to his ear, simply said, "Milord."

As if under a spell, he placed his hand under her chin to make her rise. He noticed how small and fragile she seemed to be, as he looked down into her large blue eyes. She reached out and placed her small hand in his large one, which covered hers completely. At her touch there was that shock of recognition or déjà-vu and his heart soared as he felt free of all his problems. She was the one, the only one. He knew the beauty beneath the cape for because he saw the woman the was nestled beneath it.

Talking of small things, he did notice she avoided speaking of her heritage and abilities. So they kept to things which seemed to interest Lotus most, like the up-coming wedding. She did not seem interested in his ruling of the palace, more how he treated his people. Lotus' fascination in affairs of the Kingdom and how she could help as his Queen and sorceress made Aries feel breathtaking.

Aries loved Lotus, as she seemed to absorb everything he liked and disliked. If this were a spell of love, he no longer cared, as love fell into place at every word they spoke. She seemed to know all about him already which put him at a loss and questions unanswered. The wedding would be soon, he would find out all her secrets soon enough. Walking to the old bridge, she suddenly turned towards him and tipped her head up to look into his eyes. Lotus' voice sounded the very bells of fairies as she asked if he would order the bridge to be lowered. Aries, still caught by her loveliness, was suddenly surprised. He nodded to the guard to lower it. The guard gently placed his hand on the wheel, but with squared shoulders and loud warning to the King and lady, told how the bridge was in much need of a blacksmith and carpenter to repair. Aries, being confident this would change her mind, started to turn, only to feel the tiny hand of Lotus, adamant about being outside. Lotus, pleaded with them both that they should trust her and to please walk at the right side. Lotus thanked the guard with a small curtsey. Aries noticed his smile, ear to ear.

Yes, she was the right one, winning over all she met. Everyone inside the palace came running as the bridge lowered as it fell with a loud 'bang'. Aries looked to the guard, saw the wince, the apologetic shrug of his shoulders. Aries then looked across the rickety bridge, as dust filtered though sunlight from rusted chains and rotted wood. Aries stood ridged, watching dust settle, thinking back if this was indeed the same bridge he and his father raced across many times on their hunts. Had it been so long ago, since that fatal hunt? Had he allowed so many things go, brewing in his misery and loss.

Feeling a tug on his sleeve, he looked to see his fair golden lady wanting to move on. Aries allowed Lotus to guide him halfway across this old bridge. Only when a plank fell with a plop into the murky dark waters below did Aries shake off his thoughts of father. Aries froze in his tracks, stopping Lotus as well, for she was walking on, avoiding the missing plank, as if no concern. Aries turned toward her, "We should go back until this is patched, Milady." Lotus had a different idea. To Aries horror she sat down on the very edge of this old bridge, patting a space for him to sit. Aries' people watched in curiosity and astonishment as their King and tiny maiden sat there like children, dangling their legs over the edge.

"Milady, if I promise to fix this bridge soon, may we return to the courtyard, before we fall to the murk and muck below" pleaded Aries?

"Milord Aries, I think I can fix some things if you trust me."

Sitting, he answered, "With my life, Milady Lotus." Aries sat waiting and watching his surroundings. He had missed the sudden flash of gloom which passed across Lotus' face, before she smiled and brought forth her wand from her cloak, drawing his attention back to her.

"This water seems very dark and murky. Is it stopped from the mountain which feeds it," she asked?

Aries never even thought on it, it must be. "I shall have the servants find the dam and free the water. May we go now?" Aries was becoming more persistent.

"I shall fix it for now, but you must find the blockage to feed fresh water to keep it this way," she replied. Aries felt her warmth as she leaned into him. He watched as she waved her wand across the murky water. She chanted a few words. He watched in surprise as the moat started leisurely to alter. A moat of ugly muck started its magickal transformation. Aries transfixed on the bridge, watching bewildered as it turned slowly from muck to clear blue water. The water sparkled like a mirror with an exceptional ripple. Flowers of all colors popped up out of the blue to float lazily in the still water. Golden fish, gleaming in the sunlight, nibbled the flowers, then jumped making more ripples. It was the most hypnotizing thing Aries had ever seen. Aries and Lotus suddenly startled at a sound and glanced behind them. They watched astonished, as one of the cracks in the castle wall started to patch itself.

"You fix walls as well?"

Lotus stared at the wall in puzzlement then turned back to Aries. "That was neither me nor any of my magick, Milord." They looked at each other, pondering this new riddle, until they heard another crack and knew they were about to get wet. Lotus stood. Aries watched as she walked over the bridge, repairing planks. Old rope, turning new and like snakes, moved from one plank to the next, tightening them so not even a crack was to be seen.

A farmer working the field dropped his reins and gaped like a fish, seeing a small golden lady and the King standing in the middle of the lowered bridge, over clear blue water. The farmer silently waved to the others, gathering all to watch, as a group started to walk towards the palace. Lotus felt her mistake before she heard the sickening groan. She should have fixed the chinks in the chain first, which held this now repaired bridge, but could not hold the weight of the new wood and heavy rope.

"I need your strength, Milord." Lotus grabbed Aries large hand. Taken off guard, Aries stumbled with her to the chains, now barely holding together. Aries, feeling her power, trembled, as they held the chains of this massive bridge. Their hands were like a bond and together they mended the old bridge, bringing it new life. Polishing, watching as rust floated to the new wooden floor, leaving behind a new metal chain. The chains continued to renew themselves all the way to the top; it was then they let go. But Aries could see the golden glow; she was doing too much to impress him and was exhausted. He was about to tell her that was enough when Lotus collapsed in his arms. She immediately came to and they both looked stunned as Aries slowly let her slide to her feet. "It seems I've caused an audience out here, Milord."

Aries turned to see a small band of the community gathered together, watching this miracle with tears of joy and hope shining in their eyes. The group cheered as their once sad King picked up a small golden clad lady about the waist and swung her around with joy. Aries, look into the hood at this hidden face. Lotus' smiles of joy beamed back at him. Yes, this was the one to make his people and himself very happy indeed.

There was love in the palace, the people knew it. The word was spread of a new more powerful sorceress, who captured the Kings heart. She alone could save their King and their Kingdom. Messengers were sent all through the land telling the tale of a visitor, a powerful wizard, named Odysseus, now a resident of the palace. He would be staying to help the new sorceress in her duties. Willow helped scatter the news, cleaning up the scandal of Myst. Willow noticed the departure of Amber, at first to great elation, then premonition of imminent doom. Willow knew Amber well enough to know she would not just fade into the shadows. Amber was evil and she wanted the King for herself. Willow now feared for Lotus. She would tell Odysseus her suspicions. She and her father would watch over the happy couple closely. It would only be days before the royal wedding.

The people had not actually seen his new lady for her wrap was large and hood wide. They could see the happiness of their King; the whole Kingdom heard the King and his wife-to-be were in love.

Myst, still exhausted, was in a flurry making sure all was in order for this upcoming wedding, but helping hands were plentiful, as more and more of the peasants offered services for their King, and their mysterious future Queen. Chandeliers of heavy metal dripped in crystals, donated by the blacksmith, scented candles made of rosebuds and beeswax, decorated with garlands of flowers, complements of the locals. Guards and butlers lowered the old, massive, rusty chandelier, to be replaced by new chandeliers. Raised and anchored securely, by long sturdy ropes, they made wonderful hanging pieces of beauty and light.

Huge baskets of lacy dream pillows filled the air with lavender. Sprigs of myrtle, rosemary and angelica were tied with large white bows, a breathtaking display to hang in every available space. The largest was of a huge heart with silver bells that hung from the top.

Meanwhile; Alex and the rest of the group were shown to rooms, not as elaborate as Aries, but still a quite a showplace to rest and recover, having free run of the palace and grounds. It was maddening knowing the normal person could attain access to one's own palace. Aries made sure, before all left, he would know all secrets about his own domain.

Lotus, Myst and Vickie spent a lot of time planning the wedding. Deciding on all the colors. They found a tailor, rumored to be quick and good, and he was brought before them. His work extraordinary, he was hired on the spot.

The palace walls glimmered with sparkling white stone which, for some strange reason to Myst, were now turning pink. In the palace they were surrounded by it. Myst noticed the walls turning to a darker shade of pink every day. Another riddle to this castle.

The smith poured gold into special molds for the new matching crowns. He spent time hammering elaborate designs; each crown had numerous points, which was tipped off by a garnets; a gold and red rope of fine twisted wool lay in waiting, for the fasting; many corks were being inspected in the wine cellars under the kitchen, which would burst forth from the stems of wine bottles on this fine occasion.

Aries, Alex and Nathaniel did what they did best. They stayed out of the way of the women. Spyder seemed to spend a lot of time with Willow and Sarpeden. One fine day he saw the wizard's inquisitive look, tipping his head and with a sly smile, he never missed a step.

Odysseus smiled back knowing there was no dragon, which lured him to those caverns. Lotus had to remind him once more, a dragon was an excellent sitter for young ones, but Odysseus knew they were not so young. He pondered this boy becoming one with his family.

The men tended to follow their noses, which was predictable for men-could always be found in the kitchen area to partake of food and wine. It was there the men could be found amongst the smells of dill breads, basil chickens and cheerful laughter as everyone peeled potatoes in a gleeful competition of whose peeling would be the longest. Wine spiked with lemon balm and sage tugged at every tankard.

It was the dancing girls who drew the crowd. Amber was one of many dancers, only she was under a glamour spell. She looked so stunning that night no one had known her. She danced alongside the other dancers and paid very close attention to Aries. Alex leaned into to Aries and just had to ask if he could borrow these girls for his wedding party. Aries was amused these men were so impressed with the palace girls. In the west it was tradition to party for several nights before your wedding and Aries was more pleased with their reactions than the party itself.

Sheer chiffon skirts swirled, low cut tops wavered and jingled, as the men partook of fine wine, food and women. Long, fair hair flowed, bellies wiggled in odd ways, as the women danced in seductive conduct in front of them. Alex, Nathaniel and Aries laughed at Spyder's first unattached party; he was noticeably mesmerized at the girl's talents. Spyder sat cross-legged on a table, looking at just the belly as if carrying on a conversation. He watched, eating grapes one at a time, slowly, very slowly. The dancer bumped his nose with her jeweled belly-button then giggled when he looked up in confusion as if suddenly realizing this moving belly had a face as well.

"Yes, my friends, I shall bring talent and good wine to your wedding," boasted Aries, happier than he had ever been. The transformation was amazing. "Although, this North does not seem to have the sense of humor as our West and your Myst just might not turn up to the wedding or, worse yet, she might turn you into a toad the bards shall sing about for a very long time." Aries continued, "Once upon a time there was a Prince." They all roared at Aries humor.

"Aye, you may have the best wine, for it is light and tastes of the spring, my father will love it and the talents of the west," Alex toasted with a smile and raised a brow. "As for my Myst, I cannot say, except I wish not to be a toad." Alex seemed to be in thought, then laughed with the rest. "Well, I did not come all this way to be a toad and she knows that," Alex assured them. "Just in case, let's not invite a bard to this party." All the men laughed even louder and enjoyed the rest of the night without a care.

CHAPTER 7

Secrets and Betrayals

Aries head started to feel the effects of his boasts of good wine and beautiful women, as he made his way to his rooms, a fog of dreams invading his mind. So clear and vivid, holding Lotus in his arms, after their wedding night. He staggered to the edge of his bed sitting quickly, looking out into the clear night, closing his eyes, allowing the sweet scent of the winds as they swirled though the open window, carrying freshness of new hope. The spring winds burst through his window, only to put him into a daze, hitting him with a force, as he collapsed upon his bed in a semi-unconscious state.

It was then, through the concealed door, Amber slithered in like a snake to see if the potion the wizard gave her had time to take effect. Amber, being close enough to Aries at this inane merrymaking, with a flick of her wrist, swiftly slipped the potion into his wine then moved on, out of sight, to observe his every move. She loved him in her own manner; he was handsome, strong and held power within his hands. As his Queen she would be the stronger companion and want for naught. With guarded eyes she approached him slowly. The potion took its grand time as she watched him at the celebration. Amber lifted his large hand and, without delay, he pulled her secure against him. At first she struggled in surprise as he tried once more to reach out and pull her on top of him. Amber was having second thoughts; if she were caught with the drugged King it would mean imprisonment, or worse yet, even death. Amber looked down at the small vial of potion, turning it over in hesitancy. Her head snapped up in rage as a sweet whispered word came from her adored King. Just one word, whispered in heat and passion, "Lotus."

Amber pushed back in the revulsion she felt, as he called out for his Lotus, his love. Trying to pull herself together, in a soft and luring voice, she comforted him by saying, "Milord, you know I am shy, we must be hushed and deliberate if you are in need of an heir." Amber smiled at him in revenge, before she downed the additional potion, it burned like brandy down her throat, almost gagging her. She felt it warm her abdomen. Yes, now she would be with the King's child and the scandal of the palace, but this was the price she must pay to get her way. Once sure she was with child, how easy to kill the Queen, then step into the Queen's place and make their newborn child a valid Prince. In her own sick mind she saw them happy together. Amber played the part of his new bride well, pretending to be the shy, demure, timid little girl in her rouse.

Aries breath was hot upon her skin as he murmured words of love to his new dream bride. He ran his large, calloused hands over her soft skin making her tremble in pleasure.

Under the enchanted spell of love, Aries was surrounded in a silky cloud of golden hair. It felt as though every strand caressed him as he gazed up into Lotus's eyes. Her skin was soft and bronze, her lips looked as if full of wine, the temptation to kiss her too much. They made love, long, hard love, like Amber never had from him before.

She was in great pleasure one moment, yet, in a fury the next, thinking of what he had held back from her all this time. Finally, she was pleased and surprised, as she got what she wanted; the sudden rush as he pushed hard well inside her. The warmth of him as it rushed into her, the release of his heir. She was now in total elation and control, knowing, without doubt, she now was the first to carry his child.

Aries fell into deep contented sleep, just as the wizard said he would. The shock of what he'd done would come when he found her tearful final letter, that she had wrote the night before, stating how much this final night with him had meant to her. She would keep this night in her heart and promised this secret remain between them. He would hear no more from her unless she bore his heir. If, with child, she would send a message of her needs. Amber donned her clothes quickly, leaving the tear stained letter placed in his bed, heavily laden with her signature perfume. Finally, with a superior smirk of vengeance and one last look at his smiling face, she left him in his imaginings, knowing they were of his precious Lotus.

Amber headed steadily for the shelter of the dark forest once more. She knew he would look for her with rage at what she'd done. It would be evident he was drugged and tricked, but this was the only way she could have him and live in the comfort she had become accustomed and, once with child, he could not reject her. Deep in thought, she walked along the narrow fairy path, well lit in the moonlight, batting at the low hanging branches. She came to where the trail stopped, at a majestic oak, gnarled and almost face-like. Suddenly, feeling her now shaking legs, she sat on the stump next to this large tree to ponder what she'd done. Her hand, on impulse, went to her stomach as if to feel the new life which MUST be growing. Wrapping her cloak close around her, Amber watched the low laying mist hover over the mossy rocks, near the bubbling creek, reveling in the thought of bearing the next King. She wallowed still in the feel of Aries' warm arms around her, giving her the loving feel, then frowned, for she knew he thought her to be his Lotus. "Why couldn't he love me in this manner?" she whispered on the ghostly wind, only to hear an owl cry back in answer.

As she stood, she felt the last of Aries warmth leave her, leaving her cold and emotionally sapped, but the deed was done. She ambled down the small bank to this babbling creek to clean up. The water ran clear and sparkled in the moonlight, babbling a captivating song, as it rushed over small river rocks. After tearing off a piece of her cloak and wiping down both legs, she then nonchalantly tossed the soiled cloth into the running stream, turning her back to the misty creek, not knowing she just made a vital mistake. Walking to a large tree, Amber moved the moss across the old rough bark and simply disappeared inside.

Aries woke with a great smile and immense headache. His head still in a foggy dream, struggling its way to realism. He stretched out only to feel a bit strange, for his legs were a bit stiff as were his arms, as if he were in a battle of such. The dream so real, so alive, moving beneath him, still depleted from the long love making session, even his muscles almost trembled. He was rising at the thought of this fiery dream and then he smelled it. That fragrance, it was Amber's, the taste in his mouth was bitter. He had been drugged! What had he done? Struggling to think through the fog, trying to remember, he recalled the festivities and one particular dancer who got very close, but not that close. Hell, close enough to his drink though! Could it have been her in disguise? She was not that clever, unless she had help.

He searched the divan in dismay for signs of recent passionate love-making, for stains, anything. It had to be a dream, no, for it was now a nightmare. If this was not a hallucination then he did what he said he would never do with a concubine. What if she was with child? Aries just gave her the opportunity for a child and to bring shame on him and his beloved Queen as he scanned his chambers; he found his clothes haphazardly tossed here and there. Panic raced though him as he tried to recall exactly what had transpired. Covered in sweat that smelled of sweet taint and with that sickening perfume of hers, he was about to retch when panic raced through his brain. His hand hit a piece of paper, it rustled as he grabbed it up in anger. It was the letter left for him to find.

Aries broke the seal of the letter, immediately seeing through this diversion, for this was not a fresh seal. He held the wax pot; it was cold as stone. He then used some of his ink, dipping his quill and scribed a letter upon this same parchment-not even close. This letter was unquestionably written well before he was drugged and not after, that witch! He felt ill as he scanned the lines. That wench, what had she done? He knew in his heart she planned for his bastard child and a part of his throne. She was only a dancer, a mere concubine, thinking herself in love with him. With whom was she cavorting with for such strong potions and planning for his downfall?

Aries called the guard and asked if Amber had entered during the night. There were four possibilities of why the man said, "No." The guards were drugged, the same as he, but knowing this guard he would tell his King of this. Leaving his post or lured away, again most unlikely. Or he was paid to look the other way, another unlikely, for the guards did not care for Amber or her charade of being better than them. In fact, the guards showed devotion to Myst, protecting her from running into an unpleasant scene between the two.

What worried him most was the way Amber seemed to get in and out, lacking detection.

She had a secret way in and by powers of Myst, Odysseus and Lotus, they must find it. It was not safe for the Queen and King to be sleeping and have an assassin slit their throats during the night. They must plug these holes he was discovering. Aries was torn between anger of what transpired in his bed or that any person could steal into his room devoid of exposure. He called in his only advisor. Alex. Alex was Aries' only confident of late and always had some kind of answer.

With tousled hair and disheveled look, Alex arrived in answer to Aries message of urgent magnitude. It was much too early after a night of cavorting and Alex could not envision what could possibly be so important in such early hours. Alex, showing his powerfully built chest and dark hairs which curled over the edge of his tunic, strolled into Aries vast chamber with an un-caring yawn, tunic hanging in an unseemly way, to see a King. Alex, seeing Aries was in no better shape, walked without stopping to the liquor cabinet and drew two tankards. Walking back to Aries, he shoved one of the tankards within Aries clasp.

"Here, you look like you need it," was all Alex said. He turned, sat, kicked his feet up and asked, with a simple and calm smile, for the unexpected twist of fate. "What is it?" In concern at the look in Aries eyes, bracing himself for the worst, he moved to the edge of the bed.

Aries started, "Seems as though I had a late night guest."

Alex prodded on with a knowing smile, "and, so, was this guest female?"

"I was drugged during the amusement last night; it was a potion of love. When I awoke this morn, I am afraid I made long, passionate love with Amber." Aries handed Alex the letter.

Alex scanned a few lines then spat out his mead. "She must be in jest and I thought you had guards on your door while you slept?"

"I questioned the guards, they saw no one, nor did they hear anything. There must be a way in and out of this chamber without my awareness."

Alex was almost as aghast as Aries at this weave of events. "If there was a potion strong enough to take me down, might there also be a potion to give her a child?"

Aries looked ill. "And who the hell to ask; Myst, Lotus, Odysseus? No, never Odysseus, that man could never keep a clandestine. Amber planned this plot well with someone else. The letter, I am sure, was prearranged, for it came not from my writing table. So you see my predicament, my friend, this must remain confidential between us," Aries ended, sadly.

Alex and Aries were in agreement; Lotus would never understand or accept as true this rouse and Alex had to agree. Any woman would never understand, only two days before the nuptials, how the groom was drugged at a party by his long term concubine and was now quite possibly with his child. Alex now felt the pressure, for this information could get out of hand and cause a postponement or maybe call off the wedding, putting Myst back into the wedding plans and this could not happen. Thinking fast, "Amber disappeared, unless she is with child, correct?" Alex inquired.

"That is what the letter states," Aries said.

"Well, my friend, I deem we should leave it at that," Alex answered, in a matter of fact way. "You know women; they are as a rule, not very understanding or pardoning. I would let this go unless it must come up. Maybe Amber cannot be with child, or something could happen to her, perchance a miscarriage, you never know. But the one thing we both recognize is she is devilish and not to be trusted. I would not worry, until it is time to do so."

"So, I should not be honest to Lotus before we wed?" Aries was torn.

"No, do not tell anything. Do not say anything until needed, is my counsel." This was Alex's best advice to Aries, along with bathing and changing the linens, as they downed the last of the mead. Alex left Aries to decide what to do.

While Aries and Alex had their troubles, Lotus was also having second thoughts. Lotus, fearing the peasants would stumble on to the truth she'd once been the novice of their own evil wizard Belisma, horrified her. It was her worst nightmare and she was having vicious dreams. She would awake, wet in perspiration, screaming out Belisma's name. She also was in quandary to tell Aries now or after the fasting of hands? She knew she could not hide it forever. If not the awakening of her dreams, he would certainly see the scars upon her back. How could she be untrue to him about her entire past?

Myst heard these terrible dreams many times and had run to comfort her during the worst of them. She also knew Aries would ultimately find out the truth of her past with Belisma. Myst and the rest tried their best to reassure her, but Lotus was so over wrought with guilt she was becoming ill. Myst thought it best Lotus tell Aries soon, surely he would understand.

"Secrets are a dangerous thing to keep, especially from your own folk," Myst told her, as she patted her hand in self-belief and comfort. "If he truly loves you, nothing can stand in your way." Myst ended looking up towards Alex. Now it was Alex who felt some pressure, as he heard these words from his own beloved. Should he tell her now of Aries' secret, what about his own powers? Should he tell her or take his own advice and just wait and, worse yet, should he tell her about his own connection between him and Amber? He decided on the wait.

CHAPTER 8

Finding the Grove
and the Investigation

Willow discovered something new. Spyder, jumping on a nearby rock with a flash of fire in his eyes, started on this elaborate tale. Willow had to smother her giggles, then was silent. Lotus, unaware Willow was entertaining, was making her way down to visit Willow and Sarpeden, with sandwiches and a delicacy for their golden companion. Lotus was brought up short by Spyder's voice. "It is a legendary story of a statuette of Aries' stepmother, who is suppose to stand in a secret glen within spittin' distance, or so is said," Spyder started in a low tone. "An admirer of the Queen was in the process to make a great creation the like no one could ever know. He was a simple carpenter, who inherited a great gift of magick. Of course no one knows how one inherits gifts of such, thoughts of the mind and all, but even this simple carpenter, in fact, thought he had inherited the magick so he could prevail over the Queens heart."

Willow sat with rapt attention, watching his every move, pulling her knees up to her chest. Spyder thinking she looked 'the little fairy', sitting there on the rock, listening to his every word, as he continued. Lotus stood transfixed, standing on the other side of the stone wall, listening.

She, too, heard this tale, but always shrugged it off as lore.

"It is said this once friendly carpenter inherited a book from his Uncle who was a dark wizard. It was not long before town people started to notice the influence of the dark arts coming over him. He stopped coming to play with the children as he usually did; teaching them to whittle carvings and sing silly tales. He became a hermit, starting his own grove, growing his own trees and creating magickal seeds. They said he could carve things from the hardest of wood, using only his hands and a song. He was commissioned by the King to make this statue as a legacy to the Queen and her wonderful garden, but he had other ideas and one was to win her heart. As the carpenter worked his hands over the body of this statue, molding her, shaping her, it became more and more clear he would never give her up. He fell in love with his own creation!"

Spyder approached Willow with a menacing look, raising an eyebrow as if the villain, and continued on with his scary tale. "He became possessive; once caught saying," Spyder then yelled out, "If I cannot have you, then no one shall!" Lotus and Willow jumped as his voice went from whisper to maddening yell. Sarpeden looked up at this moderate interruption. "The story ends wretchedly, milady." Spyder dipped his head, as if in sorrow, seeing he had a rapt audience and decided to end his tale on the final sad note. "It seems the old man went quite mad with his creations, making one after another to protect her in this glen, until he, himself could not enter.

After many sorrowful attempts to reclaim her from the glen and failing, he simply vanished. Where he went I cannot say, but some believe he still lurks, hoping someone with more power than he will claim her. Then he shall steal her away, into the night, just as a lost lover. No one knows for sure what happened and all are in fear to find out, as this tale has run long and strong for many a-year. Many who have heard this tale search for this glen, sometimes in shining armor. Though they go into the glen to become rich men, they never seem to return." Spyder ended, a sad look upon his face. He had even given himself the shivers.

Spyder was in disbelief when Willow asked, almost breathlessly, "So, where is this place?"

"Though this statue might be worth a lot, its curse is not worth your life," he told Willow. "A foggy glen, a madman, a curse, you cannot be serious!" Spyder, becoming panicked, paced the cavern, eyeing Sarpeden, seeing from her expression he would get no help in this direction.

"What I wish to know, my dear Spyder, is what you are doing hanging with tavern ruffians, listening to drunken folly?" Willow wagged a finger to an unsuspecting Spyder.

"Well, it ain't like we be married," Spyder said, slapping his knee in evident merriment. "Ol' Odysseus would be turnin' me into a toad for sure," he ended.

"I could turn you into a toad. And what is wrong with us being wed?" Willow looked almost crushed, as her eyes glazing over with unshed tears.

"I didn't mean I would never wish for you, my dear Willow, but I am far from good standing in your father's eyes." Spyder, seeing the dejection on her face, consoled her in the only manner he knew; changing the focus back to where they started. "Willow, it is said this glen is magick with a dark wizard, and he went mad worshipping this statue like his personal Goddess or mayhap a real woman. It's also said this statue's not carved, but molded by his hands from special wood. Isn't that the silliest thing ya ever heard?"

"Where is it, this statue? Did they steal it and sell it?" Willow was back on track.

"They're afraid to even look for it; say it's protected by some sorta magickal golems." By the look in Willow's eyes, Spyder knew he'd woven this tale too well. "Ya can't be serious! We could get ourselves killed! It's just a tale the locals tell to run fools in circles of a chase."

"We shall look anyway and if we find it or any danger, we shall come back to alert the others. Besides, I know a little magick of my own." Willow had spoken. They would look for this illusionary statue first thing on the dawn.

"Can we be takin' the monster with us?" Spyder looked towards an unresponsive Sarpeden, who also knew something, but she was not telling.

"She cannot be seen quite yet," Willow said with a satisfied snort behind her.

"See, even old draggy here don't be believing it's real. I should've never told aye," Spyder stuttered, looking at Sarpeden once more for help.

Willow, smiling, poked Spyder's shoulder. "What's wrong; you cowardly?"

Taking offense, Spyder stood and bowed towards Willow. "I shall be here on the dawn, milady." And he sauntered from the grotto.

Lotus, like a ghost, slipped back to the tower, hands wringing in uncertainty. She could not involve Odysseus and Myst without drawing them away from the castle, causing suspicion to Aries. She felt Willow and Spyder were now in grave danger, and with Willow's slight magick, maybe she could protect them in some manner; but she could not go alone. If Spyder's story was half true, she felt she should tag along, just in case, but with whom? Aries would only stop her from going, so . . . Alex! He would be her best bet. She donned her robe and eased her way down to see him. It was late and most unsuitable, but under these state of affairs Lotus felt she must be the carrier of this pertinent information. Suspicious of the palace couriers to deliver a message of this proposition, she knew she must be the one to hand deliver it herself for the wellbeing of the children. Lotus paused a brief second, hand in mid-air, gathering her strength and composure before rapping softly upon Alex's door.

Without delay he yanked open the door, almost as if he sensed her existence. They stood staring at one another for a brief, most uncomfortable, instant. Lotus, eyes wide in surprise at his unexpected appearance, securely clutched her golden robes. Alex stood in the doorway, a candlelit glow behind him, ruffled dark hair, wide bared chest, cheroot hanging from a firm mouth, and a clear stunned look upon his chiseled face.

"Milady, you certainly caught me off guard this fine eve. I was preparing for the servant to bring more of this superb wine." Alex held up an empty jug, as if she'd not believe him. Lotus was quickly caught off guard when Alex reached out, grabbing the front of her robes and roughly yanked her into his room. She was unceremoniously pushed flat behind the door against the rough hard stone. A firm finger pressed her lips for silence. She squirmed when his hand went lower to her neck, almost reaching her chest. Looking down Lotus saw Alex made no move to close the door, but held it open with his knee. She stilled under his hand, feeling the heat of it firmly pressed against her chest, but her eyes protested his insolence.

"Post haste, my boy," Alex shouted, to the servant boy down the corridor, as he carefully carried the bread and wine requested. Lotus took in a deep breath and held it, not wanting to be exposed in Alex's rooms after dark, in her robes. It would be a most upsetting state of affairs for them both. Alex felt her take that deep breath. He also felt the shock wave run through his hand and into his body, thinking only of soft supple skin and a curl of golden hair as it slithered down the back of his hand, so soft, silk like.

Shaking himself back to reality, Alex received the serving dish, allowing the boy to set the tray on a nearby table. Alex could see Lotus watching through the crack of the door as he casually tossed a coin in the general direction of the boy. It also did not escape his attention of his hand still resting upon her chest and her red face. He quickly thought of removing it from its warmth, but then it might be best to keep her where she was, until the boy left, but Lotus felt his hand lingered too long, become too warm and she now felt branded by another man. Oh, what a mess she had got herself into this time!

"That will be all for tonight, my lad," he commanded, then slammed the door in a 'do not bother me for the rest of the night' gesture, releasing this golden one like a hot coal.

'What the hell was he doing and why was she even here?' Alex turned to don a nearby robe, only to turn back towards Lotus with a grim look on his face. "Are you out of your mind, what if Aries or Myst happened by or a gossiping servant for that matter?"

"It is for that reason I came to you first, in secret." Lotus then sat quickly near him, too near for his comfort, and softly spoke of things to soon transpire on the morrow.

Alex felt warm sitting this close to her, her whispering into his ear, leaning against him. Suddenly he rose and walked to the beveled mirror, looking at himself very carefully, and for a very long time.

"What are you doing, milord?" Lotus asked, mystified.

"Just wondering, why is it me everyone seems to run to when they have a secret or a very large problem?" He turned to Lotus with perfectly raised brow, stating, "Or both."

"Does that mean you are in agreement or nay?" Lotus asked.

"Yes, I will rally with you, we shall pursue them, and pull them out if needed. Happy now, Princess?"

"Yes." Lotus slipped gladly from his room, leaving a wary Alex behind wondering what had Spyder's web caught and was it going to cost love or life.

Willow and Spyder searched many nearby glens and found nothing save deer, rabbits and other mundane fauna, which were annoyed by their passing. They found themselves far from civilization in the wooded hills, where only seasoned woodmen tread when game was scarce. Trees here were ancient bastions of their species, most being as large in diameter as a man was tall. Vines hung thick in the limbs and brambles of berry bushes making the going slow and, at times, painful. Not to mention the thick fog which clung to these higher hills well into the late morning.

It was in the clinging midst of such a fog Willow stumbled over an arm-sized tree root snaking its way from the ground. Wind milling her arms, she fell forward, nearly clutching raspberry bushes on her way down, but she fortunately fell away in time. Her relief was short lived though, as the ground gave way suddenly under her. Raspberry bushes plummeted into the unknown, not two feet away from her head, as soil under her body crumbled away in a shower as she saw the edge of a precipice from the veil of fog.

Only with reactions honed from a life such as Spyder lived, was he able to dive forward and catch Willow by her narrow ankle. Spyder's, now falling beneath the fog, realized Willow lay on the edge of a cliff. The thick woods ended abruptly. Beyond the tree line he saw a huge emptiness, as the fog so clogged the forest, now settled into whatever lay below. Willow lay very still on the brink, hair dangling forward into nothingness, hands pitched out before her, as if she could push away what she thought would easily come. Streams of loosened dirt and gravel rolled past her chin and from under her arms, as she watched the stones steadily getting smaller until they vanished into a bank of fog below. Only after Spyder began to pull her slowly away from the edge did she realize the swirling fog was now settling into a beautiful glen far below.

Spyder whistled softly as the two crouched there at the edge of the cliff. The mid-morning sun beat down upon the glen, doing its best to burn away the waves of fog clinging to the trees below. It seemed this valley trapped moist sea air, combining with any dry air coming in from the west, as it tried unsuccessfully to escape to the sea. The result was a rainbow effect in the billowing clouds of the glen. The sun glinted off the moist air, spreading out in a prism effect.

Eyes straining, Willow looked far into the glen, as it seemingly appeared out of this void of fog. A wide arch of trees spread across the valley in a very unnatural formation. No, trees did not grow naturally in geometric formations. The fog billowed, as if pushed by a light breeze, not a limb swayed in the woods, not a single limb, not a branch, not even a leaf. Further, not a sound reached her ears from below. Behind her, crickets chirped, birds sang, a breeze pushed dead limbs against tree trunks, the woods alive with sound. Below, the valley was silent as a tomb. A slight smile crossed her features, yes, this would almost certainly be a grand adventure.

"We found it!" was all she said.

Discovering this glen was far from miraculous. Without climbing gear, no one would be simply dropping into the glen itself. It seemed Spyder was way ahead of Willow in his thinking. "If we follow the cliff edge, keeping it in sight, but not too close, mind ye," he began, "we mightn't be findin' a place to climb down and not be bustin' our noggins."

Willow could hardly argue with the logic, especially since she didn't have any better ideas, so the pair set out. It seemed the raspberry bushes preferred to grow right along the cliff edge and this made the going even slower.

Spyder hacked away at the offending growths as Willow picked berries, edible roots and tubers. Who knew how long they would be at the glen, exploring? Why be careless with their food-stock?

She nearly filled a third bag when her footing gave way again. She slid down the rocky slope, mentally grumbling about her bad luck. The ride lasted but a second, which seemed to be an eternity in her mind, as she was followed by a wave of dirt and gravel. There she sat in a cloud of dust. Pulling herself up, she looked down now ankle deep in loose, muddy soil. Worse yet, Spyder appeared hovering over her back at the top of the ravine smiling broadly.

"I see you found a quicker way out" he shouted down to her. Kicking away several of the rocks half buried in the slope, she made her own avalanche, but he deftly rode the wave of loosened soil down to the bottom.

"This part of the gorge seems quite slippery and steep," he said, with a smirk, "but you found a very quick way down."

Willow snorted and rubbed at her sensitive ankle. "Let's go on then" the rest of the way was indeed treacherous as they slipped along on moss covered rocks that severed as stepping stone across the water.

It was then that Spyder lost his footing and splashed knee deep into the rapidly moving stream. Spyder seemed almost offended by the water touching him, as if it was the worst thing to happen to him in months and he quickly leaped from the water.

"What's the matter, allergic to water" she asked, giggling behind her hand?

The stream wound through the hills and made wondrous waterfalls where the sounds echoed loudly, emptying into the sea. So engaged were these two in this sudden change of light and sound; Willow and Spyder never once knew of Alex and Lotus following behind-always just out of sight, but not out of ear shot.

The walls of the ravine sloped away from this area like a cup, leaving no way into the grove itself, but to push aside a particularly dense patch of these offending cat tails and finally ending up into the valley.

The valley spread out before them like a painted picture. Near them, a patch of stinging nettles, but beyond was pure beauty. Flowers of innumerable variety made a low blanket upon the valley floor. Birch trees showed off white trunks, only to be out done by flowering Dogwood. Oak of inestimable age towered into the sky forming a near complete canopy above the heads of their Ash, Maple and Pine brothers. Wild Roses perfumed the air along with Lilac, Honeysuckle and Jasmine. A true feast for the senses.

Willow stepped from the muddy water onto solid ground and promptly sat. Spyder followed suit and scanned the canyon walls, while Willow wiped her boots clean on the sparkling moss.

"Notice the color of these leaves, Willow?" Spyder whispered quietly.

Willow turned and examined the tree. "Yeah they're green."

"No, they are a perfect green and trunks look like people . . ." he started.

Willow finally took better notice. "Yes, perfect flowers, perfect scent, perfect leaves; how very odd."

Willow hurriedly replaced her wet boots, as they skirted outside the woods, quietly debating about this strange formation in the trees. It wasn't long before the shapes became more and more easily spotted and they began to feel uneasy, as if they were no longer alone, but within a crowd. All if they were silent sentinels, watching, waiting

"Look at this place. I've never seen the like of it. I feel like we're being watched."

'Wasn't that rose bush to the right of the maple sapling before? No, could not be possible.' They were merely exhausted. It was then she spied it, just clear of the maple sapling. A cabin lay nestled beyond a thicket of birches, fairly close to the rock face walls on this side of the glen.

Spyder spied it too. There was no light from within and no sign of habitation for quite some time. Oh, this was not good, not good at all. Willow's eyes lit up.

She whispered to Spyder, "Come, let us look a bit closer."

"Darn, woman, I wish you wouldn't startle me! Breathing right down my neck and in a whisper like you was—I thought I'd been had." Spyder wasn't sure. None of this seemed right. Still, maybe there was something worth his time in there. The decision now made; in a matter of a heartbeat Willow quietly slipped past him, heading forward toward the cabin. He wanted to shout, to tell her to let him go first, but if there were someone or something in there. He followed, stepping in footprints he found in the carpet of low-growing Phlox she imprinted.

Willow had gone nearly ten yards before Spyder caught up to her. She stood right around the corner of the cabin, in full sight of the front windows. Spyder caught her shoulder and pressed her firmly against him as they backed away.

"SHHHH" he pressed a finger to his lips, at her surprised look.

"SHHH, yourself," she hissed back. "Look at the ground. No prints, no paths worn bare from walking. No one's been around here in a long time."

Spyder had been peering around the tree trunk at the house while she chastised him. Indeed, she was probably right. The windows were shuttered; the porch sagged heavily to one side.

Taking a deep breath, they held hands, approaching the cabin with caution. The front door hung awkward and slightly open, as if one of the hinges could no long bear the weight. Flower beds along the porch overgrown with weeds, though tall tiger lilies still bloomed through the onslaught. Spyder took the lead with Willow close in tow as they approached the house. He grimaced as his weight caused planks on the porch to groan, but nothing seemed to care. Willow peeked through a small break in the shutters as Spyder looked in through an opening caused by the door hinge giving up its job. What they saw was the same . . . lots of dust.

It was a full two stories tall with what seemed to be attic space above. The front door led into a spacious living and dining room dominated by a bulky oak table with four chairs set about. A great fireplace set in the left hand wall complete with a mantel and vast hearth. Both front windows let light spill into this room, but only because the curtains, once rich and made of satin, were split from age and lack of care.

Willow spoke first. "Well, it's obvious he did not live alone, at least not for long."

The living room held a split stairway leading both right then left, probably to the bedrooms. A passage led further back into the house in both directions. Spyder looked down the halls. He could see the kitchen closest so he decided to start there. Willow decided to start her investigation upstairs while Spyder explored the lower level. The stairs were quite solid, not being beaten by the elements, like the front door and shutters.

A smooth hand rail led away and ended with a carved flourish in a dirty, very dusty room. Against the far wall sat an oversized bed, bedside table, a footlocker at its end. A large walnut wardrobe sat in the far right hand corner, matching dresser not far from it. Wedged in the wall were intricate engraved pegs for hanging fine clothes. On either side of the headboard hung small unlit lamps, over half full of oil. The bed itself covered with a thick looking, but rather unadorned coverlet, seemed to squish like it was filled with goose down, not with straw or other such roughness.

The wardrobe and dresser contained nothing but mundane clothing, dusty now from abandonment. Willow examined the carved walnut footlocker next, but securely locked with no key evident, she'd no chance to open it. She did, however, find a small ornately carved wooden box and a tiny oil painting set in a silver frame complete with glass covering. The painting, probably once exquisite, now so dusty all she could make out was the form of a woman. It must be the portrait of his love, the Queen! The woman was, indeed, beautiful in form, though her face would be forever clouded by dust from inside the frame. She shrugged and replaced the picture, and examined the box. The box itself, made from some deep brown, rich wood, the feel of solid rock when touched. The carvings were remarkable and had to have been done by an absolute master in order to make this hard wood look so beautiful. The lid lifted easily off to show some strange wood shavings, some dusty old seeds and what appeared to be a fey flute! Now THIS was a rare find; an instrument with which he created his magick. Willow placed the box in her backpack to show Myst later.

Downstairs, Spyder was getting frustrated. The right hand doorway led into a very commonplace and very boring kitchen. A large fireplace, capable of holding an equally large stew pot, set in the outer wall. The stew pot was held on a thick metal pole, hinged into the side of the stonework, so it could be pulled out of the fire if needed and swung back in to continue cooking. It was about the only thing interesting in the whole blamed room. A ordinary ash can, sat beside the fireplace, with equally ordinary fire utensils.

Cabinets surrounded the walls containing very old, very dusty foodstuffs in the upper cabinets, while the lower cabinets contained cooking utensils and dishes. His eyes sparkled as he examined a single, large, very well made knife with full tang and curious balance. This knife found its way into his possessions as he went along.

Spyder took about two minutes probing, before leaving to explore the other doorway. This room was a study or den. There were several book shelves in here, but not enough to call the room a library. A smaller table sat at an angle between the shelves in the corner. On the desk sat three corked vials which looked like ink and a single open book. Spyder pocketed the ink vials along with the book. The desk also contained three drawers, which Spyder jimmied open with his newly acquired knife. Inside he found a large stack of paper weighted down at the edges with six unused candles, an ornate tinder box containing flint, and some fluff from some bird feathers.

All of these things found their way into Spyder's voluminous pouches, though the book did not want to fit into anything easily. He'd managed to stuff it into his largest pouch when he heard Willow descending the stairs. They walked hand in hand down the hallway into the back of the house. It emptied into a room larger than the upstairs bedroom taking up the entire back half of the house including the yard. This room was a marvel of engineering; not because the total ceiling was made of various panes of glass, but because the walls seemed to be made of stained and leaded glass. The first impression Willow was awe ... shelves held an array of oddly labeled jars, decanters of brightly colored liquids which sparkled in the sunlight, even though the glass was dusty. Who knew how many pots, bottles, and boxes were stored in this room of life.

Woodworking tools, planers, hand-held drills of some sort, and sanders of all kinds and sizes were held on yet another shelf. A workbench sat to one side of the room, containing an array of alchemical apparatus, braziers which would heat glass pots, allowing steam into this glass tube which carried it to this distilling device . . . which sent the liquid to ... it hurt her head thinking about it. Then she spied the cupboard filled with pigeon holes and rolled parchment. 'Plans?' she wondered.

Spyder first thought about the room itself. The walls should not be strong enough to support the ceiling. Not only that, these glass walls were also held up shelves which were holding many pounds of various ... stuff. Outside, an overgrown flower bed held a dozen or so huge sunflowers, which stubbornly refused to give in to the Venca vine trying to choke it out. Rose bushes climbed up the outside of the glass walls clear onto the roof, exploding roses, the size of a small melon, in colors so brilliant they looked like they had been freshly painted.

"This man sure knew how to grow weird things," Spyder commented.

"You have no idea," Willow said, as she stuffed all the parchments. She was silent for a moment until the awareness hit her. She turned to Spyder. "This is not glass; you can see the impression of a grain to it." The walls and ceiling were made of some kind of clear wood! "I get a funny feeling about this room," was all Willow could say.

"He was not just an artisan, but a very powerful wizard as well. Actually, from what I can tell, he grew plants and wood then shaped them with his feelings, but most important, with magick," Willow explained.

"If'n he was so very powerful, why would he just up and leave? I have seen no body, no grave. Why would he leave and not take his prized possessions?" Spyder snorted, "Course, with his powers and all, it wouldn't be hard ta find a commission among the other wizards'.

Willow giggled, "I didn't say wealth, and I said prized possessions. Upstairs, on the bedside table, is a painting of his only true love, the Queen. The only other things I found were some dusty clothes and an old locked footlocker, still locked. Willow turned in time to see Spyder mounting the stairs; he'd heard nothing of her speculations.

Upstairs, Spyder found much the same thing that Willow had, but he saw it differently. The wardrobe was still filled with clothes, but contained no secret compartments. The dresser also held clothes, but had no valuables hidden beneath. The bed, while soft and filled with feathers, held nothing under the mattress. Frowning, Spyder went to work on the lock.

She waited until his short return. "Find anything good my thief?" she shouted.

Spyder harrumphed, "Just junk."

Something in his voice told Willow different. His pouches and backpack had more bulges than normal, especially the one which spewed forth the corner of a very large ledger or book of some sort.

She took a deep breath and stepped one foot back into the glass room, stepping boldly into the room and walked over to the table. She dumped out some of food and repacked her bag with vile after vile of fertilizer? We will see, she thought.

CHAPTER 9

Willows in Trouble and Lotus Shows New Powers

"Something seems amiss here," said Alex, startling Lotus, whom he ordered to await his return from searching the back of the cabin. Lotus became quite uneasy; he had disappeared for some time now. "What do you think this is?" Alex asked, holding up an unfinished piece of wood. "I found it tossed out back, along with some other unfinished work."

Lotus, very intrigued, inspected this statue of a woman playing a harp, her poise perfect, as if she were about to play. She wondered why the wizard had tossed it, needing but color with pigment, a final touch to be perfect. It was quite beautiful, but overly large for the normal home. "Wonder what his plans were for it?" Lotus asked, running her hands over the smooth wood. She got a tingling sensation, almost as if . . . "Oh, my, this is beautiful." About to approach Alex, with her thoughts to take this piece back with them, unexpectedly, she caught the look in his eye. She lowered her voice, stunned, as he carefully reached for his blade.

Alex almost dropped the harp, sensing danger about. Lotus picked up on his relatively strange actions, his intellect of dread and peril, as she reached for his sword.

Afraid to move, "Alex . . . ?" she started to ask, but he already knew the question to come.

"Never touch my sword; never ask me about powers or special gifts. If you ever see any, it is between us or we shall go no further! Understand?"

Lotus nodded. So Alex, too, had his secrets. How extraordinary to chose the one man who was hiding something. "I chose very well. I sense we both have secrets."

"Don't look so smug, milady, for we may depart this life today, we shall take our little secrets with us. You shall follow my guidance or Aries shall have my head. Even with my powers, I do not think I can grow another."

Lotus looked at Alex as if he could. What did growing heads have to do with this? She had little time to think on Alex's secrets when Willow and Spyder exited the lodge, carrying more out than they went in with. This was not good at all, especially when they turned off the trail toward the palace, deciding on walking into the shadowy orchard itself. Lotus looked to Alex with concern, watching in horror, as the two stepped off the trail. Halfway, the orchards undergrowth seemed to suck them in, covering them in shadows and gloom.

Alex, troubled at losing them within the dark gloom, glanced to Lotus, sitting there; wringing her hands in desperation . . . neither knew what to do. Actually there was nothing they could do at this point; less they reveal themselves to these two misfits. So they held back, waiting with fear and trepidation.

Willow, noticing the foliage growing thicker and dark, slowed her stride, watchful for any movement. "Thought you wanted to see inside the orchard?" Spyder asked, pulling her along.

"You don't see it? Feel it in the air?"

"See what? Feel what?" Spyder slowed his steps, noticing her uneasy gait. He trusted her instincts. If something was wrong, they should be away from this place. Willow thought she saw a dark shadow creep closer, her first thought was, 'Run!' They saw the large grove for what it was, full of seed and nature, and yet void of any life . . . no song of bird. Willow stood straight; this must surely be a deception in her mind. "If you do not see it; then it must not be there. Let's go and take a look." But Willow could not shake the feeling they were being stalked; Spyder, too, now ill at ease.

They walked inside an orchard full of unbelievable mysticism. Sunrays streaked across the wide spectrum of gleaming moss and fungi. It bounced like prisms of colored glass from tree to tree. Upon closer look it was not the sun, but light beaming from a collection of ripened fruit pods. They glowed, almost ready to burst with seed. The pods hung low on bended branches in a variety of spectacular colors. The flowers here were plentiful, mostly grown in a hedge witches garden. Witches highly recommended many of these plants for strong brews and potions, being extremely poisonous plants. They stood tall in the midst of other pretties you did not dare to eat; foxglove, oak moss and mistletoe.

Crystals and stone work were also well placed. 'So, this artisan did work dark magick.' "Defensive magick," Willow whispered. "Used in negative spells, powerful words poured within these stones. Depending on the spell, or curse, they may last eternally." The first thing to catch their eye was an owl. Upon first look it seemed ordinary, but a closer glance showed this bird carved. His eyes glared at them intently and seemed to follow their every move. Willow now knew they stood in a trap. She eased her way back, turning towards Spyder.

"See the owl?" Willow whispered. "Somehow this carving is active, here to warn trespassers of impending kismet."

"It's a statue," Spyder said. He walked straight to it and thumped its chest with a nonchalant gesture. "See, this is nothing but wood."

"Stop, do not move. Owls are notorious for staring at you for equality. Many lost souls have been raised by these creatures. They fly over their graves. These birds can blight you with the curse of darkness always to be the hunted. I think now is the time to turn back my friend," she finished. Spyder did not argue.

Willow caught her breath and turned for one last look in admiration of this complexity; she missed the movement under her feet, entrance by all this beauty. Spyder knew he should have made her go with him, when she felt fear, from the very first. Spyder, too, took in one last glance of this wondrous place. He turned back to see a white faced Willow frozen in her tracks. He heard the small snap of a twig and thought nothing of it; after all, they were in an orchard where branches and twigs fell all the time. "Well, are we leaving?" Spyder cast his gaze from her whitened face, now seeing a panicked look in her eyes. He followed her eyes down to see what looked like a root. Thinking she was trying to scare him, he reached down to remove it, but before he touched it, it moved! He fell back realizing it was not a root, but a wooden snake the size of his thumb, wrapping its way around her. Both knew they were in over their heads and did the only thing they could ... scream ... hoping someone above or nearby would hear their pleas.

"That is our entrance cue," Alex said, unceremoniously grabbing Lotus by her hand. He had all but carried her into the depths of the orchard, leaving the statue behind . . . for now. Alex pulled a fretful Lotus through the course ruble. She heard the song of death as Alex unsheathed his blade. It was then she heard the cries of the others and was caught up in only reaching those she had come to love, whom were now in need. Alex slowed his pace as his sword glowed with impeding danger.

Lotus knew this man was indeed of magickal quality. "We must go to them!" Lotus hastened in front of Alex in great urgency.

"Are you daft woman? As I told you before, you shall wait on my escort! I will not answer to Aries about your hasty death. Look around you girl . . . get your senses!"

"What is this place? All this glitter dust and charged energy? We must get them and leave post haste, milord!" Lotus, clearly panic-stricken, noticed for the first time the bars of lead intermittingly struck into the ground. Alex held Lotus close as he tried to hear the couple who were in need, over the sound of her heavy breathing, of her heart pounding. It was then he honed in on the now smothered gasps of Willow, the tired and exhausted ranting and ravings of Spyder.

"That's them alright. I would know that panicked squeal from any distance. How the blast do we get to them safely now, milady?" Alex was close, too close; Lotus could feel the warmth of his breath as he spoke. She had never been with a man and she found it uncomfortable molded next to his hard body. She could almost feel his blood rushing through his veins.

"First, milord, I suggest you let me go; I promise not to run away," she panted, finishing in a gasp.

Alex released her immediately, not realizing he held her so firm. "Aries may want my head after all, when I enlighten how I have bruised his wife to be, and then Odysseus. How will I ever explain to my old comrade the harm I allowed us to be in without his counsel, embarking without telling at least him?"

"I am certain all will be forgiven, once they learn we have rescued our friends, Milord. Besides 'tis only early afternoon, certainly we are not missed yet." Lotus stumbled away. But Alex was not the only one who worried, for back at the palace they were all missed, initially by Aries, searching for his love, Lotus. With no result finding her, Aries, without delay, went to seek out Myst, who was missing a certain Alex. They both went to the west tower only to be questioned by an angry Odysseus on the whereabouts of his daughter and that no-good Spyder!

Aries gathered his guards to find them at all costs. He even called for his horse, as Nate and Vickie joined in the search. Myst went to the tower to scour for them. A huffy Odysseus went deep into the caverns to question one gold dragon, who knew, but was under oath not to tell.

It was Lotus who came up with a clear and sensible idea. "What does wood fear the most? Fire, but, then again, there are these lead pillars which still stand tall. I would say these pillars keep the golems alive and protect this forest. They could also be a communicator." Another gasp for air hit their ears, a curse and a hacking sound. "We have a warrior, a power mage and a tiny spell caster, but I fear there will be no need to go at all if we wait much longer." Lotus was in fear.

"I concur. Just stay close and remember, if we can be of no service here, we must depart them . . . understood?" Alex set his jaw. Lotus could not be of this same faith. Barely touching the ground, they rushed into the orchard. Lotus pulled back like a frightened kitten. "What is it?" Alex asked, ready for an encounter. Alex felt his sword starting to warm by his side. He looked to Lotus, who could, with mage wisdom, feel the rare and evil magick which cracked throughout the air. They both knew the warning signs of danger ahead, behind, surrounding them.

"This madman made and grew all this with magick and wood. Let us hope it is not fire-resistant," Lotus said, as she and Alex called softly on the winds for the lost couple. Within seconds came the response they feared the most; the panicked voice of Spyder,

"Over here! Hurry! We are surrounded!" The shout came within the forest edge; deeper in the grove than Alex and Lotus wanted to go. Alex charged forward and in his haste; he dragged an unbalance Lotus. He pulled her through ruble and thickets, scratching her skin, tearing her dress. He pulled up short at the sight of Willow's entrapment. Alex cocked his head at this strange turn of events, forgetting Lotus, being dragged in his wake like a rag doll.

At this sudden stop, Lotus, in the process of shaking many a cocklebur from her cloak, took a deep breath, ready to tell him of her feelings of this rough treatment. She managed a few words of complaint. "Do you always treat women in this fashion when saving people? If so, my magickal friend, your people skills need be worked on!"

Alex set his hands upon her shoulders and roughly swung Lotus about to directly in front of him, to assess the situation as well. There was Spyder hacking away with all his might, dagger flailing at his opponent, which seemed to be wooden snake. Alex, totally confused, watched Spyder do a little jig about this animated wood, which only seemed to tighten more. He did the only thing he could possibly think of, saying, "Well, Milady, go work your magick." Alex courteously bowed toward the track leading to the mass confusion.

Lotus did not as much as blink. "I doubt gravely we have much precious time," he whispered in her ear, pointing to this oddity in front of them. Lotus once more felt his hot breath. "I believe this more your area in magick than mine, milady. After all, this was your scheme to come to this place, to become their savior. Seems this needs a touch more than a mere sword will prove to be." She made her way to Willow with wide-eyed caution, taking in all around her. She was brought up short, seeing a now unconscious Willow, in the embrace of a wooden snake. Lotus tried to clear her thoughts, to think on what needed to be done. Gathering in her surroundings, she took in everything from a frozen Spyder, now guarded by the stillness of a large black wolf. Her eyes were drawn to the wolves as they followed her every move. How unnatural, how odd; she must clear her mind to free herself and her friends. Lotus's eyes snapped open as to what Alex had just said.

"This needs a touch more than a mere sword. I fear we fell off of our little world of Vardania." A 'touch' . . . just the clue she required! With deep concentration and determination she gathered herself as one. First things first as Lotus checked Willow. Her faint breathing told her, as long as Willow did not struggle, the snake would not squeeze. She clasped her hands together, rubbing them fiercely, then lay them upon the wooden snake. Using a burning touch would not put Willow's life in peril, but instantly make this snake rear its head slowly in pain.

Lotus took a step away. One and all saw her smoldering handprints on its body, heard the hissing noise as it burned into the wood. The snake started to recoil into the cold earth, leaving behind his prey to rest; a limp Willow, gasping, sobbing for breath.

Spyder eased Willow into his arms, ignoring the wolf, which glared intently at this new confrontation. The wolf's sudden show of aggression caught them all off guard. With lips curled back, white bone fanged teeth bared, the eyes moved in a lurking way, searching for the weakest point before pouncing on this small party.

"What are these things protecting?" yelled Alex.

The figurine of old Kings Wife; "The Queen of all statues," answered Willow, with a small croak. A crack filled the air as wood strained to move and the wolf decided on the weakest possible foe; Willow. Intent on landing on a protective Spyder, who was shielding a fragile Willow with his own body, the wolf arched into the air.

Aloft, in a graceful death strike, the wolf, like a bolt from the blue, was hit by sudden lightening. Though the same crackling sound as usually made the ragged edges of yellow and red blaze of fire was incorrect. This fire bolt of force exploded from Lotus's hands. All looked at the now charred and flaming wolf to Lotus, who was just as stunned as the rest.

"I feared for their lives, panicked, and it just happened," she managed to falter out.

"Well, keep your hands downward till we figure out what that was, and how you can command it," muttered Alex, sniffing the charred, blackened, still smoldering dog. "Good enough for a campfire, but by no means a real wolf for eating. Smells like fried wolf though."

Lotus swiftly put her hands to her sides, a combination of revelation and elation of what she could do now. She held much power, then a frown it hit her face, as she thought back on this situation. She recalled Odysseus saying something of making her a new kind of magick. Power which now grew within her, magick which must not be hidden away from Aries before the nuptials, their very lives may be impacted by her alteration. Shook from her thoughts, Lotus felt the wind lift through her hair. They were not out of danger.

CHAPTER 10

The Fight for Their Lives

Lotus took in her environment, inspecting the odd pods which hung low and full on smooth branches, yet staying her distance. Somehow, some way, she knew the forewarning secret language, as did Willow, written on the steel pillars.

"Gather to me," Lotus commanded, without question they gathered to her side. Lotus, motivated to shield those now under her charge, created an orb of protection, dispeller of magick, which circled and gyrated around them. The sight from within this orb was incredible. They stood awed by the vision of pods splitting open, setting seeds free floating, much like blowing winds across a meadow of fuzzy headed dandelions. However, as each minuscule seedling hit Lotus's sphere they heard a crackle and saw these were not simply seedlings, but tiny tufted darts with pointed ends and lethal aim. "I do hope this blows over rapidly, I grow drained, holding us all in the interior of this field." Lotus sounded weary. Willow held her hand gently in fear, trust and faith, hoping, perchance, she could transform some of her magick into Lotus, making her stronger.

Soon they could hear the beating of these darts, as they looked out through Lotus's amber shield, which swirled in transfixion of red and gold. Even the tiny foliage was spiked and blade sharp. How long Lotus could hold this barrier for them, they wondered, then, it stopped. Lotus dropped her hands in tired relief, but the blush in her face made clear how the link between mind and energy had been demanding. Limping, staggering, helping each other, they made their way to the edge of this dark forest, almost into the core.

"The earth here is more dominant deep within this glen, the element more fertile and rich for all plant life, which it needs for greater growth. Combining the element of air, which is a courier of nature, it can sense a differentiation in charisma. The fog ensnared here stimulated by the lead standing stone, a negative force, which I deem tells these golems there is a shift within this mad garden. Earth, water, and air have all sustained this grove, but left it to one very vulnerable element, fire. This wizard was very cleaver in the creations, which now surrounds us, interweaving these powers. He found a way to mold and bend wood with his hands, then to protect his prized possession. Wooden golem's work perfectly to protect this place, I must say," Lotus ended.

"So, how do we kill them all?" Alex stood, asking the question on everyone's mind.

Willow was uncomfortable. "I feel we should not kill it, but neutralize it in some fashion . . . somehow." She looked around at all the un-believers, except for Lotus.

With dull sarcasm, "Now what do we do, little sorceress?" Alex asked of Lotus.

"What does your fancy blade do, anyway? I have a plan to seek out this legendary statuette of the Queen, that is, if it really exists." Lotus gave Alex an expectant look.

"Naught of your distress at this position, milady, of what my sword was planned for, let us get on with the task of finding the cursed item and take our leave of this place," was his only offer.

She saw the set of his jaw, the lift of his finely arched eyebrow. Lotus did not query him further.

Spyder, wanting to be a fraction in this tight group and expressive about all secrets known, started on a tangent. "Milady, Sir Alex is a proud man and does not wish to brag, but you see that there sword . . ." Those were Spyder's last words, before he was snatched up by his tunic and shook about "When I need your help I shall be sure to ask for it!" Alex lowered the startled boy to the ground.

"From what I feel within this area of the forest," Lotus continued, "we are dealing with the un-dead. We attract these creatures by movement and sound. These creations are intelligent; therefore, they only have one function; to guard as the wizard programmed them to."

Alex, mystified and alert, asked, "So, how do we kill the un-dead, if already dead?"

"We use what wood is most afraid of, fire and light," said Lotus. "Regrettably, these protectors of the glen were interwoven with magickal defenses against trespassers. Therefore, they will shield themselves against us; we must be prepared for such a show of aggression." Lotus took the lead. "Stop," Lotus stopped them with just the halt of a whispered tone. They all saw where she pointed; a nest of spiders, brown and grays of the wood. The wooden spiders skittered forward on legs made of wood and some sort of vine. A heavy coating of moss lay across their backs, giving them the appearance of a typical hairy spider, but these were hardly typical arachnids. The size of large dogs, they poured out of their nest in waves which made it hard to see just how many there were. A dozen, perhaps a full score of the things, belched out of the nest, legs clattering together in a horrid cacophony of clicks, while their tread almost soundless, in the moss and plant covered forest floor.

His sword already unsheathed, Alex was the first to react, stepping boldly forward to meet the mass of spiders alone if need be. "Stay behind me, milady." He motioned to Lotus. "I shall hold off the onslaught whilst you retreat." The spiders were coming at a large rate. All minds branched off in different guidelines. Alex tried to watch as everyone spread out. He saw Spyder offer Willow a hand, boosting her deftly to the lower limbs of a tree, then melt away into the taller branches.

The first wave of wooden arachnids marched toward Alex, when he heard Lotus begin her incantation. She spoke in whispered tones, gradually becoming a swirling vortex of raw power, formed and molded by her will. Within seconds, a wall of blazing flames erupted from the ground around the spider's nest, circling it, catching a few unlucky foes in the conflagration. Those spiders caught in the fire burst instantly into flame, though they seemed not to notice. They continued, leaving little flaming footprints in the plants as they tread on. Finally, the greenery was wet enough to subdue the fire, leaving a smoky trail, puffing out any remaining fire.

Horrified her spell had done nothing, but make the foes even more dangerous, Lotus saw the spiders stop . . . their delicate legs burning to wiggling stumps. They dropped on the greenery smoking and popping until the fire went out, leaving nothing but charred, motionless, logs.

Alex took this all in without so much as an upward glance at the flaming inferno. One of the spiders crouched low before him, its bulbous body sinking down atop its back pair of legs. As he expected, the arachnid launched itself at him, coming in at head level. Alex side stepped slightly and turned. He allowed himself just offline from the attack, and chopped at the flying thing. Hit just between its body and thorax segments, the spider flew headlong into a nearby tree, but quickly righted its body as best it could and continued its attack. Alex blanched. His sword should have split the thing neatly in two! All it managed was a nasty gouge in the spider's carapace, not much more than a normal woodcutter's axe could have done. There was little time to ponder such, as the next creature leapt upon him.

Spyder moved slow, trying hard not to move the various plants around him. If Lotus was correct and these things were activated by movement, he could be almost invisible to them. He moved like a shadow, slinking sideways as he kept his eyes trained on the battle before him, eyes peering between the tops of this plant and the next. He counted sixteen, clear of the nest, before Lotus so deftly walled them in.

The heat became more intense as he circled behind the masses, between them and their nest, enough so foliage blackened several feet away from the flames. He was relieved to see the spell could not reach the greenery around the far side of the nest, catching all the underbrush afire. This way he could easily flank the foes!

Seeing how well these things leaped, Willow quickly pulled her feet up under her . . . any dangling digits could be fodder! What was she to do? Spyder had vanished and Alex fought for his life just below her. How could he hold off all these things? Eventually they would overwhelm him and Lotus would be next. Then what? Then they would climb the tree and she would be swarmed! She shook these thoughts from her mind for gloom and doom never helped anyone. But what could she do? These things were undead! How could she kill something not alive to begin with? Maybe she didn't have to; maybe she could just help Alex do it! Willow summoned her own magic and forced her will into her words. The magick poured from her. She began shaking her hands back and forth. The weeds on the other side of the clearing began to sway in rhythm of her hands. It was working! She was doing it!

Alex knew he was in trouble. His sword's magickally sharp blade was stopped short by these equally magick wooden creatures. He could easily beat the things away as they leapt on him, but they always scuttled back, with little more than a chip gouged out of their underbellies. One spider, chipped now three times, jumped at him from his left, Alex turned to beat it back again. This time though, another spider jumped him from behind as he turned. Alex spun around, his forehead throbbing with the sense of impending danger and managed an overhand cut, ducking low under the spider as it passed above him. His swing a bit wild, coming more from desperation than skill, he missed the spider's body completely. He did, however, manage to hit its legs as it flew by; the delicate legs sent spinning to one side as the body spun off to the other. The legs! The legs were vulnerable! If there just weren't so damned many of them!

Spyder felt a pang of guilt, watching Alex bravely battling the small hoard of things, to little avail. Maybe if he had stood with the great warrior. No, he would do his companion much better with the element of surprise on his side. After all, what good was a dagger against creatures even Alex seemingly could not slay! He stopped, quietly emptying out his largest sack, dumping candlesticks, paper, and a copper bowl out onto a large patch of moss. His impromptu weapon now ready, Spyder crept behind one of the smaller foes and pounced. The struggle over in just a few seconds, the nimble thief swept his foe's legs into a bunch and simply forced its body into the sack. It squirmed around like a turtle on its back, but Spyder had it. A quick loop of leather, a knot, one foe now vanquished. However, the tussle alerted three more to his presence

Lotus felt the sweat beading on her brow as her will kept the flames burning, but burning under her control. To drop the spell now she could risk it going out of control. Even so, the fire field had done its job; any spiders encircled by her flame had been burned, rendered legless by now. She released the magick back into the nothingness from which she called it and leaned back against a tree trunk, her will severely taxed, her mind growing quite weary.

Alex watched in amazement as the spiders split their forces away from him. One third of them scuttled off, wildly swaying on his right. He hoped Spyder was not so clumsy as to give them a target. The things were getting more and more organized it seemed, attacking from two different directions at once, circling him and attacking at two different heights. The intelligence was impossible from normal spiders. A pack of wolves would be hard pressed to use this kind of organization. Could they have been created with this level of intelligence? Alex had doubt; something had to be controlling them.

Willow watched her spell draw five spiders from Alex, but she didn't even care. Her happiness drained away her concentration, ending the spell; she had done a good job. Now, maybe, just maybe, Alex could take them out.

Spyder drew the large knife he found in the cabin and twirled it in his hand, spinning with unconscious grace, until the blade was in high palm. He threw it at the nearest spider, hoping to pin its body to the ground. Even as he drew out his two fighting daggers, he saw the attack had been for naught. The knife simply stuck in the spider's wooden side. At least it made it hard for the damned thing to walk!

Alex dropped another spider by hacking away all four legs on one side. This was the eighth spider he crippled, though they managed to hurt him right back. He was bleeding from a dozen small wounds, mostly from the vicious fangs and mandibles of these wooden spiders. The wooden teeth were easily the equal of steel in both strength and in sharpness, though it did seem to lose some tensile strength when forged, or carved, to thin pieces. It would make fine arrow shafts though. His stray thoughts cost him in blood as a spider bit into his ankle. The thing was still fighting even after severing every leg on one side of its body! With a scowl, Alex stomped down on the thing with all his weight, rewarded by a crunching sound similar to small branches when shattered into kindling.

Spyder was in trouble. Bleeding from several gashes in his arms and legs, his cuts were drawing blood. The wooden spiders showed little effect on their bodies from his attacks. He had retreated unconsciously as he fought, and found himself with his back to a tree, three spiders spread out in front of him in a wide arch. At least now they could not circle and attack from two sides. One spider jumped at him again, but Spyder was ready. He slashed both daggers across in front of him to deflect the attack and watched the tumbling thing smash into a tree beside him. This move crushed three of the spider's legs, but it righted itself in the undergrowth and came back into place hobbling only slightly.

Alex near laughter, as he surveyed the scene around him, as a dozen of them squirmed around him in legless dance. Some had a few legs remaining and they now turned circles in the dirt, working their functioning legs, but rooted to the spot by the weight of their legless sides. He turned his attention to the spiders lurking in the weeds at his right. They seemed to be hunting for whatever it was which moved in the weeds and paid him almost no attention as he approached. Alex cleaved downward at the nearest one, severing all its legs in two swift strokes. The others did not seem to notice, and just milled around the area. Alex finished the remaining spiders with leg slicing strokes, leaving them to lie helpless in the weeds.

Lotus watched as Alex dismembered the remaining spiders like a woodsman with an axe. A horrible thought crossed her mind. 'What if these things could grow new legs?' They were made of wood, maybe some fertilizer and a good rain would make them good as new. She decided a simple fire spell was not beyond her. Speaking the words, she sparked a flame to life on one of the spider's severed legs. She then took this flame and applied it to every wounded and legless spider in turn; charring their bodies. Willow joined in her task, making sure their enemies were truly down for the count.

Meanwhile, Spyder was at a stalemate. He may not be able to hurt these spiders much, but neither could they get their fangs through his own guard. It was a matter of which party would get reinforcements first. He watched the spiders closely. They stopped moving altogether, not even bobbing up and down on their spindly legs. He chanced turning his head, allowing his peripheral vision to keep his foes in check. He thought he saw movement from the corner of his eye several times during the battle, just a hint of something over in those trees. Up high, like a giant bird perched in the branches. Now, as he studied those trees, not a flinch of movement did he see.

After he finished the remaining spiders, Alex took a deep breath and scanned the area; where the blaze was Spyder? It took almost a minute for him to creep around and find the thief besieged by a trio of wounded, but still standing, spiders.

Spyder spied Alex round a shielding tree. He knew Alex tried his best to be silent, but to his ears each step Alex took was like the pounding of a hammer to an anvil. Spyder smiled slightly as Alex put his finger to his lips, signing for Spyder to be quiet. Alex got within ten feet when Spyder saw his foes crouch down. Steeling his muscles, Spyder waited for the attack, but the spiders jumped backward upon the sneaking Alex. At the same time, Spyder saw opportunity to join in the fray and he did quite well, as they both worked jointly, slicing away at the aggressive spiders.

One spider retreated, sliding silently through the trees, toward a strange motion. Once within ten yards, Spyder saw the source of the motion, as did Willow and Lotus, who had decided on reversing the negative flow through the arched steel.

A giant of a man, once crouched in the lower boughs of a huge oak tree, now stood watching the battle Alex was giving the wooden spiders. He must be all of fifteen feet tall, a glossy green-gold in color, much like the spiders themselves. As if this were not enough to give pause, the giant held to the bough with two huge hands, holding the limbs above with an additional pair of arms. The upper arms seemed to be flitting back and forth with movements of the spiders below, as if the spiders were pulling on his hands like puppet strings. Spyder's fears were solidified as this giant turned away from him and motioned with one of his upper arms, the motion sparking a pair of wooden mountain lions into the fray. Spyder went silently back to rejoin the fray with Alex, these two pumas would be ferocious foes, he would need the help. Alex dripped trickles of blood from several wounds, but the spiders were helpless before him by the time Spyder joined the fray.

Alex drew a ragged breath as the thief approached. "Please, let this be the last of them," he said, smiling at Spyder. "Except for the one you bagged."

"More company approaches from there," Spyder said, pointing. "And there is a wooden giant in the trees who seems to be directing their movements."

"Well, now, that certainly explains things. Why would spiders attack moving weeds? Why hadn't they attacked me when I attacked the same spiders from behind? This 'master' could not see them! The spiders simply attacked movement unless directed by this unseen hand. They milled around in the weeds looking for whatever moved the weeds. Meanwhile, out in the open, the spiders were attacking with the intelligence of this same master who obviously understood combat better than any normal arachnid ever could." Alex was way over Spyder's head.

A low growl, the only warning, as two large mountain lions parted the undergrowth in the middle of an attacking leap. Alex didn't need much more than a single growl. Ducking low, his sword sliced through the air, drawing a line from the puma's chin to his crotch. The slice would have killed any living cat outright, but this wooden cat simply landed behind him, leaping again.

Spyder, caught slightly off guard, managed to roll with the weight he found clinging to his chest, a pair of daggers piercing the thing's chest and belly. The puma rolled off him during the second tumble, taking one of his daggers with it, stuck in what would normally have been the creature's vitals. It turned on this annoyance, clawing and nipping at the dagger, as if a burr stuck in its fur. Spyder backed away, put his back to Alex's back, thinking these new threats could not flank them with this stance.

Alex turned just in time to see Spyder come up behind him. It was a good idea to not leave their backs exposed to attack, and Alex found a new respect for this little thief for even thinking of the maneuver.

"My daggers hardly scratch them," Spyder whispered.

"Even my sword is of little use against this enchanted wood," Alex revealed.

"Then we are in trouble deep . . ."

Scratching away the protruding dagger as if an annoying flea, the mountain lion hissed terribly at the duo standing between it and its companion. Both of them began circling at the same time, turning like hands on a clock, in perfect unison.

"Aye, and if they are being directed by intelligence better than their own animal counterparts . . ." Alex began.

"I can't see why we battle them at all," Spyder spouted. "If controlled by yon giant . . ."

Alex had thought of that. "True, but these cats will be on us as soon as our backs are turned."

Spyder smiled. "Then we be in need of distraction, aye?"

"Aye, and with Lotus all but drained of strength, I fear we are on our own."

Lotus and Willow finished their task, burning all the downed spiders into charred clumps of wood. Time was now to tackle the energy force itself. Lotus stood by one steel arch, Willow another, where they were first attacked. They both knew what to do and started the chant. What else could these bizarre woods send them? As if on cue, the sounds of clashing steel snapped both of their heads around, breaking their concentration, as they scurried toward the sound.

Lotus felt a lump in her throat as Alex cried out in obvious pain. Suddenly, fatigue forgotten, Lotus led Willow a merry chase through light underbrush. Occasional thickets of brambles poked and tore her dress, but Lotus pounded through like a startled rabbit, Willow darting around them in slightly less haste than her companion. Willow and Lotus wrestled through a pair of young maple saplings, looking at the battle beyond.

Alex dripped bright red rivulets of blood down his chest; deep claw marks etched his arms and legs.

Spyder was only slightly luckier. Though his arms and legs were less cut, he sported a deep wound on his shoulder that looked like he'd fallen into the steel jaws of a bear trap. His arm hung limp at his side, though he managed to hold a dagger in that hand, blade held defensively along the bone of his forearm. Alex, panting in the humid air, sword held low in both hands, stared down on what appeared to be a wooden mountain lion. A second such puma lay crushed against a tree some five feet away, it seemed the pair had done quite a bit of damage.

"Stay back," Alex shouted, as though he knew of their presence without the slightest glimpse their way. "If you move, you may draw attention. I cannot protect you both from here."

"Aye," Spyder added, "and the thing in control lay yonder, low in the boughs of yon oak trce. He may not be able to see you from there."

CHAPTER 11

The Final Battle

Lotus cared not whether she could see her target all she knew was that Spyder needed a healer, now! Quick to assess Alex, her eyes grew wide in amazement. He stood facing her, looking as though he should drop from loss of blood. There were no doubts his wounds were already healing. Once again, his secret life now exposed to others. Lotus felt his hurt, the insecurity of their reaction; what a pity to have such a gift, but feel you must hide from those you love. Yes, Lotus had chosen wisely in her companion. Angrily, she started to summon her will, drawing attention away from Alex, back to the quest at hand.

Nearby bushes, even small trees, wavered in the tumult created. Willow stood back, surprised and slightly afraid of the power she felt crawling along her spine. When the magick burst forth, it was both terrible and beautiful at once.

A walnut-sized ball of flame appeared in Lotus' outstretched palm, glowing bright red, turned blue, yellow, then nearly pure white. It streaked from her palm like a hawk diving for prey, trailing bits of crackling energy in its wake.

It hit the lower branches of the massive oak tree some thirty yards away and blossomed into a sphere of fiery energy with the force of a landslide.

The inferno lasted only a second, its fury undeniable. The force of impact blew away tree limbs, some as thick as a giants leg. Lesser limbs were simply reduced to so much ash.

The impact knocked Spyder and Alex onto their bellies, they arose to find a third of the massive oak incinerated. Tiny motes of flaming ash hovered in the air, blown about on invisible wind currents. Lotus knelt in a patch of low growing phlox and panted, chest heaving for breath, a vicious snarl still splitting her face. Her hair danced in an unseen wind, Willow backed away from her several paces. 'Now that was magick!' she thought.

Alex surveyed the scene, his recovery quick. The huge 'giant', Spyder had spied, now nowhere to be seen, perhaps incinerated by the blast. The puma lay huddled on the ground, not moving. Spyder quickly went to work, hacking away at its forepaws and gaping maw determined if it were to animate again, there would be fewer weapons to deal with. Meanwhile, Willow joined Alex going through the wreckage. Lotus caught her breath and when Spyder finished de-clawing his former foe, he too joined the group.

Not a word was said about the massive show of magickal force Lotus had unleashed, or of the fast healing of Alex, not yet, not with another potential opponent lying in wait.

Willow saw it first. "By all the Gods," was all she could manage.

The giant stood from its former perch, a full fifteen feet in height. It was a golden-green in color with patches of bark adorning its chest, legs, and arms. Small clumps of living plant growth sprouted from the top of its head and shoulders, more at its ankles. Its toes and feet looked like roots of a tree. Aside from its four arms, it could easily pass for a forest giant from afar, but up close one could easily make out the wood grain in its torso and limbs. Tiny pools of some gooey liquid oozed out several small cracks in its side and chest. Sap, perhaps?

Spyder couldn't help but lean in and examine the largish patch of pure gold bark covering its upper chest. He was running his fingers over it like a jeweler appraising the value of an unknown material when it opened its eyes. Willow immediately screamed as though a mouse just climbed her stockings. Alex pushed Lotus behind him, waving his sword between him and the now rising giant. This wooden giant seemed not to care his look locked on Lotus, eyes uncaring and uncompromising. He then scanned around only briefly, engaging each party member separately and then bent at the knees. He picked up a massive tree branch blown from the oak behind him. He then launched into action.

Its first move was use this large branch as a battering ram to push Willow some five feet away and left her tumbling to the ground.

Alex gave a guttural shout engaging the brute. His first wild swing meant not to injure, but as a feint, trying to force the giant to turn away from Lotus, but its attack was intent on her.

Alex managed to parry the attack by spinning in a full circle. The blow was such his entire upper body trembled from the force. Spyder managed to get behind the brute and launched his own attack at the thing's back knees. The dagger blades did not bite deeply into this enchanted wood, but it did shove the thing slightly off balance. Looking back to spy this new threat, the giant simply held his staff at ready with its upper arms while reaching down with one of its lower pair. It snagged Spyder by the collar, hurling him nearly ten feet away, where the nimble thief managed to roll back to his feet. "Ye'll have to do better than that, tree!" the thief shouted, but it didn't seem to notice. Instead, it used the great reach of its upper arms to push its staff at Alex, who tried to circle to its left. Alex parried the blow and managed to hack away most of the brush which adorned the business end of its weapon. This did not seem to bother the silent giant, as he simply spun the staff from a horizontal attack into a vertical one in mid attack. No longer soundless, it spoke its first words. "My name is 'Hollow'. I wish to know why you have come to destroy my paradise, and I want the answer from the woman there." The tree pointed straight at Lotus.

"We have come for 'The Queen' of this glen."

"You cannot have her, for she is under my protection." With a great sweep of his wooden arms, "You have destroyed the field that helped me in her defense, the field outside of my reach. So now, mortals, deal with my wraith!"

Alex, ready for this onslaught, side stepped, blocking the blow with his blade. The wood crashed down on the enchanted blade with punishing force, enough to sever the end of the staff completely.

Lotus managed to back away from the melee, unsure exactly what to do. 'If a fireball didn't kill this thing outright, then what . . . 'Alex stepped back, he knew now he was not dealing with some mindless automaton, but the leader of them. This was a creature of great magick; a creature, not only animated by magick, but intelligence and emotions as well.

Alex was going to use every bit of training, experience and every bit of his gifts, just to survive this. He had to, for if he should fall, Lotus would be at the mercy of this unnatural glen. Alex was certain Lotus was too defenseless, as he saw her call upon her will again, ignoring the searing pain at her temples. From outstretched hands burst a swarm of blue-white darts, each one streaking unerringly between him and the wooden golem.

The magic missiles peppered into the thing's chest, causing it to stagger back slightly with each impact. As their glow faded they left only tiny trickles of sap which began healing over with some form of tree bark. In all, it managed to turn the giants' attention, once again, to Lotus.

Alex saw Spyder take this opening to dive in behind the giant, but this time he did not try to slash him. For the second time this day, Alex found a new respect for the little man. He rushed the giant as it turned toward Lotus and drove forward with all the strength of his massive legs. The giant, forced back by this new attack, shoved its staff between him and Alex, but the attack was not meant to draw blood or sap. It was meant simply to stagger him back into the crouching Spyder. The wooden giant did fall across Spyder in perfection and Spyder sprung instantly, hacking away the downed foe with all his might. Alex joined him, raining blow upon blow into the creature's torso. The creature was neither fast nor agile enough to deflect the blows and soon a dozen or more streaks of deep red sap began spilling onto the ground. It tried in vain to parry with its staff and lower set of arms, but wherever it moved, another blow landed elsewhere.

Spyder gasped for air, tired and desperate. His blows were doing almost nothing, not even going exactly where he aimed. He hoped what he lacked in precision would be made up in sheer number of blows. But it wasn't. As Spyder paused to take a breath, the creature struck, reaching out with one of its lower arms, catching the thief by the throat. Spyder's eyes grew into huge orbs of panic as he felt his very life being squeezed from him.

Alex, too, was weary. He'd thrown dozens of blows, only to find his best cuts draw only a miniscule trickle of its sap. Now the giant was using Spyder as a makeshift shield, holding him between itself and Alex's sword, as it rose again to its feet.

'Sorry Willow,' Spyder thought, as blackness enveloped him. 'I'd much liked to spend more time with ye, mayhap a great deal more time . . .' Alex saw Spyder go limp in the giant's grasp. Though overcome with outrage and horror he couldn't fight with the body of his friend being used as a shield against him! He felt useless!

Willow picked herself slowly out of a field of tiger lilies, just in time to see Spyder hanging limply in the giant's grasp. "NO!"

Lotus saw and launched yet another spell at the seemingly invulnerable wooden golem. A simple spell of pure force meant to push an adversary or hit it with a slight impact. However, her spells were being powered not by just ability and training, but full power of emotion, desperation and rage. The force blast hit the wooden man full in the chest with sledgehammer impact.

The giant stumbled backward, unconsciously dropping Spyder and its staff, clutching its chest of bark with all four of its great hands. Alex saw his opening and stepped in. Becoming a whirling circle of death, Alex spun in a dance of attacks that would have fallen any number of human foes in the first seconds of battle. The giant seemed not to even notice. It did not even defend itself, allowing Alex to draw deeper and deeper cuts across its legs and torso as it continued to clutch its chest.

Willow rushed right by Alex, to her fallen thief. He looked like a crumpled piece of parchment, limbs sprawled in every which direction. Though shallow, he still drew breath, his chest rising and falling in an even rhythm. He would live, that is, if any of them could stop this monster before them. Willow was about to take up a pair of daggers, lying at Spyder's side, when she was grabbed around the waist. Her turn to be crushed in his massive wooden arms had come.

When Spyder came to, the sight he saw was mind-boggling. Willow, being squeezed almost to death, was too much for him to bear; he vowed a silent vow to give his life, if need be, to vanquish this beast killing his little Willow.

Alex stopped in mid-slash when he saw his blows were ineffectual. But, he had also seen what effect Lotus' blow had upon him. Turning his sword in his grip, Alex began using the flat of the blade and concentrated his blows on the giant's chest.

Willow could not get close to the monster. Alex was crashing heavy blows across its chest, as it tried desperately to slap away the sword with its bare hands. But those hands were so large . . . its arms so long! If she were to get closer, the thing would just slap her away like a gnat.

Alex saw Spyder, his unexpected ally, as he darted in and out, trying to find the things body, an actual body part where he could deliver a blow. He side-stepped and spun, drawing the creature away from him, forcing it to turn its back to him to keep him safe.

Spyder saw this not as an attempt to keep him safe, but as a way for him to unleash his full fury. He let out a low-pitched growl, like a true warrior in a battle, and jumped upon the thing's back, raining down blows with his dagger. The wooden golem was now disoriented with something on its back, protruding from its shoulder. A strange man stood before him, slashing with a sword, actually wounding him. A sorceress unleashed fire attacks upon him, sending magick crashing into his chest. The giant became confused, desperate.

The golem reached back with all four of its arms, releasing Willow, in his attempt to dislodge the thing clinging to it. Alex saw another hole and pounced with waning energy, using the flat of his blade again. The first blow had results as the creature staggered, yet again. The second blow struck a patch of armoring tree bark on its chest. The third knocked the same piece of armor askew.

Alex saw it. Beneath a large piece of bark, adorning the golem's chest, a pumping, pulsating orb of wood, the thing's heart wood. He had a chance. The golem nearly berserk, its protective chest plate now dislodged, revealing its only true vulnerable part. The thing, on its back, was relentless, holding on like some starving tick, as Alex rained blow upon blow, forcing it to dispense more and more healing sap.

Spyder, in a rage, saw nothing, but his enemy. He rode it, became part of it. He looped his legs around the thing's lower shoulders; put his feet behind it, on its back. From this position his weight was steady, balanced, while his hands were free to drive daggers into this walking chunk of hardwood. He saw he was making massive wounds. With every new blow, another piece chipped away. Every attack deepened another crack.

"It's chest!" Alex screamed. "Concentrate on its chest!"

Spyder heard someone talking to him, as if whispering from down a long tunnel. He couldn't quite make it out. "Chest, what about his chest" he yelled back? Its chest was certainly stronger than its back." Spyder raised himself upright and saw Alex far below him, trying desperately to parry the golem's flailing arms away. His mouth moved like he was yelling, but Spyder heard nothing. All Spyder cared about was the thing he held in a death grip with his legs. He looked at it as it turned its head to look at the warrior. He saw fear in its eyes, he saw desperation there. Spyder saw the growing patch of thick red sap oozing from beneath a dislodged piece of tree bark on its chest.

Alex almost died instantly, as a crushing blow from one of the golem's wildly flailing arms whipped by his head, a mere fraction of an inch away. He was slowing; every reserve of energy spent, pain beginning to seep through the rush of adrenaline. His arms felt like someone had tied stones to them. His wounds would heal, of course, given time. He had certainly healed from worse, but if he couldn't down this seemingly tireless golem, it would not matter. It would simply wait until he could no longer lift his sword and pound him into a bloody pulp. Then it happened. One ham-sized fist found its way through Alex's guard, pounding into his chest with such force; it blew all of the air from his chest. He dropped to one knee, sucking for air; as the golem loomed over him, bending down to reach the smaller foe with a look of unholy glee in its heartless eyes. When the golem bent forward, Spyder was not ready for it. His legs slipped from under its arm and he careened forward over its head. Dropping one dagger, he grasped for any handhold; one of its arms, a growing bit of leaves, a piece of bark.

Alex watched in horror as Spyder tumbled forward over the golem's shoulders, turning in mid-air, flailing for his sense of balance. He caught something on its chest and hung there, eye-to-eye, with the un-living, yet animated master of the glen. Its eyes were smoldering now. Earlier, the thing seemed dead as a pile of firewood. Now, at the moment of its certain victory, it seemed as alive as any other horrid monster awakened him from a long nightmare. Spyder found him-self not afraid at all. He was enraged. His heart trembled as he clung from one of these branches. He looked down on his friends, Lotus by Willows side, Alex bent down on one knee, powerless to go on.

The golem's eyes went wide as he turned his attention from his downed foe to the wisp of a thing once clinging to its back. It was a frail looking mortal he could crush with just one of his hands. And it had nearly fallen off him, only barely catching onto one of his branches. The thing chuckled and in a booming voice said, "You're dead little man. You're all dead." On that, Spyder let go of the branch and caught onto his chest plate. With sudden dismay, the giant saw the glint of this 'little mans' dagger plunge downward, towards his unprotected heartwood. That was the last thing it would ever see.

Spyder smiled as he drove the dagger downward into the things heart with all his strength, shouting, "No, my friend . . . you're dead!" Without the benefit of warrior training of any kind, he relied on pure hatred and vengeance to power his stroke. The blow landed just off center, in the things pulsating heart, with enough force the dagger blade snapped at the hilt, the protecting armor breaking away from its chest. He swung up as the great monster began to fall, riding a wild ride the remaining ten feet to the ground and landing in a heap at Alex's feet.

Alex drew up, regaining his footing, as the giant clutched its now ruined chest. He pulled himself away from harm and watched as the thing lost color immediately, turning from burnished gold to sickly rust. The various patches of living leaves on the body withered and dropped away like dead leaves in a windstorm. Then it began to crack. The noise, nearly deafening from a distance of now ten feet, grew louder, as the wood split in a dozen places at once. Grain pulled away from itself, parting in spiral patterns across its torso.

Alex dragged Lotus and Willow to safety as the golem started, bit by bit, to fall apart. The arms gave way first, shattering like a hot rock tossed into a pond. Then the chest burst outward in a storm of flying splinters and chunks of wood that still oozed sap. Finally, the legs gave way, snapping with a loud crack, sounding like a bolt of lightning had struck.

Spyder had killed his beast and was on his way down, hanging onto the golems head yelling, "TIMBER!" They all laughed.

CHAPTER 12

Finding the Statue

The sun startled them as it broke through the high mists, which were no longer blocked by the dark grove creatures. Where these creatures retreated was open to guess. Sunshine showered the grove in a sparkling display, dancing on the energy crystals and iron stones, exploding with great force.

Alex took this time to hide, to heal in private. Lotus, too, needed this occasion to recuperate; she found by laying in the hot sunlight her recovery was quick. Absorbing the bright rays of the sun, feeling her powers becoming stronger, she watched diligently as with a new sense of immense awareness.

Willow, oblivious of her own exhaustion as she nurtured Spyder's needs, seemed his own special hedge witch.

Lotus sat up with great strength and a clear mind. She now knew all of Alex's secrets and how Willow was truly 'totally in love' with Spyder. Lotus lay back, thinking how fortunate she was to have such companions as these. It was then Willow unexpectedly looked up as something caught her eye off in the distance. Lotus followed her gaze across the rolling glen, calling out to Alex, who came running like a charging bull.

"What now?" Alex commanded, as he looked for a new foe.

"Look." Lotus saw the frantic look in his eye. "Willow has found it."

Gathering themselves, they stared across the well lit glen. Perched precariously on the very edge of a sheer cliff, there for all to see, the figurine they searched and fought for so diligently, the figure of Aries stepmother. Lotus watched as Willow and Spyder made their way without hazard toward the cliff, then up, straight up, following the sunbeams right to this radiant statuette.

"Be wary up there, as it does not look very steady," Lotus called out to them.

Spyder looked down at Lotus as if she had just lost her mind, whispering to Willow, "Has she forgotten already what we have just been through? Now she is worried?" Giggling, they both waved to her, smiling as they reached the statue. Lotus watched in absorption, as Willow reached her destination, running her hands over this creation. Made of the same phenomenal wood this master artist had used, there she stood, the lady of the garden, as if carved that very day.

Lotus closed her eyes in meditation as Willow inspected this wood monument. Amazed as she was at picking up Willow's sensation of contact with the woodland timber, she was flabbergasted to read her thoughts. 'The litheness of the wood looks as if oiled on an everyday basis. The colors are throughout, sinking deep into the wood itself or was it a pigment at all of stain, dyed oils or paint? The artist has actually impressed it with the grain, bringing out long strokes of special colors.' Lotus picked up all this from Willow's mind.

"It is an amazing piece of art," Willow yelled down to her, as the sun followed her hand across the figurines hair. As if mesmerized, Lotus watched Willow's hand follow the grain, then both startled when the hair seemed to move. Was it a trick of the mind? Willow was still drained from Lotus transformation and worn from the recent attack; they shook off this hallucination. Having the feeling of abandoning this lady, Willow could not find it within herself to leave her, so sent Spyder down with a message.

They watched as Spyder slid quickly down the slope, unmindful of the sharp rocks in the rush to get to Lotus, looking back several times to make sure she was still there and safe.

"Willow cannot bring herself to leave the statue. So if you can levitate us outta here," Spyder spat out hastily, as he reached Lotus's side.

Lotus looked at Spyder, Willow and the heavy statue, then at Alex, with an uncertain frown. Alex saw her fears of dropping them all and opted on another method. "If you levitate yourself and the small ones, then throw a rope down, I can make sure the statue and I can be hoisted out of this glen." Lotus looked towards Alex with a grateful smile.

"I can most meekly try the lighter of the small ones, and see to your safety once we reach the top." Lotus grabbed hold of Spyder's hand, and closed her eyes; without delay, they started to ascend the ground, catching Willow on their way towards the crest. Alex thought it best to climb most the way towards the effigy. He wanted to see this unusual vision for himself, up close.

Lotus sent Spyder back for Myst, a rope, cart and driver, never taking her eyes off the lady or Alex, as he examined this strange object. It was not long before Spyder returned with a well padded wagon and a very anxious Myst. Once there, Lotus and Alex explained everything to Myst. Myst turned to Lotus and told her, "You must go home; everyone is in search of you. Be warned, he is not in the best of moods." Myst had come prepared with a rune to the palace and inside the west tower. She opened a portal, wished Lotus the best, and sent her through; at least Aries would be happy, not knowing Aries sat in the same room when Lotus stepped through. Myst then turned to Alex, "My Prince, whatever have I done for you to run away from me?"

"I went in search for a rare and beautiful treasure, such as you, Milady."

"Then you are forgiven." Myst threw her arms around his neck, almost knocking him down with a passionate kiss. Once the kiss was broken, hearing a giggling sound from Willow and a gagging sound from Spyder, Myst realized the importance of their find. She inspected this statue with great care, as if a druid were captured in the sunlight and frozen in this place. Her gown blended into the green moss, which crept across the stone shelf, holding her in place.

"Was told of me an Elvin was the artist. Well, tis Spyder's tale to tell, but I have some things to show you from this master carver's cabin".

"What happened to this smith?" asked Willow, concerned.

"No one knows for sure, he just disappeared when she died."

"Look," Myst pointed to the carving upon the figurines upper breast line, "the same outline as Aries amulet." Sparkling in the sunlit glen, there in the carving was the exact stone. Myst and Willow inspected the perfect carving and decided it indeed the same amulet he now bore, but how could that be? Myst's head was spinning. "How is it this statue made long ago, a King and a peasant woman from far away, have the same amulet?" Myst motioned for the driver of the wagon to haul up some of the sacks he carried in his farm cart. As she wrapped the rough sacks around the wood, Myst whispered into one finely carved ear. "We cannot leave you all alone when there are many people who remember you. Besides, you have a stepson I am sure you would not want to miss. Yes?" Myst ended on the question as a child to a small doll.

The statue had long, hip length hair, with a crown on top. Her eyes were almond shaped, embedded with a very light sapphire stone, fringed with long lashes, small nose, but full lips. Her face was oval, almost perfect, tilted lovingly on a swanlike neck.

Her gown fit tight with a low cut to show the amulet. The fullness of her breasts could be seen before the gown cut away in a tight fit, showing her tight waist, full hips, then flared out in the back to a slight train which rippled still with moss.

Her hands were carved small and delicate, but it was the ring that caught all attention. It was the only article not of wood, but of metal, a supposed gift from the smith.

Willow touched the figure and instead of the inflexible feeling wood gave, it was as if someone came day after day to oil and care for it, making it supple, yielding to the touch, almost like human skin. An eccentric feeling as if your hand went to sleep, then you felt it with your other hand. There was that suppleness, a part of you, but at the same time, detached. Almost a feeling of life, but yet . . .

CHAPTER 13

A Place for a Perfect Wedding

Once they left the grove, secreting this amazing statue in the West Tower they could all focus on a certain noble hand-fasting. Willow heard some fascinating news from an older woman who sold beautiful flowers in the market and agreed to meet her and Myst alongside the palace. Willow convinced Myst to meet with them in a hidden place at the mountain side.

"Where are you?" Myst whispered, trying to find them amongst the overgrowth on the palace fortifications.

"We are over here, shush, everyone will hear you, milady. Willow stuck out an arm, waving frantically at Myst who was about to scream, as a wild overflowing brush of vines grabbed for her.

"You frightened me!" Myst glanced at Willow and an ancient looking woman. Willow, allowing a small giggle at Myst's reaction, "Seems we have a trespasser in our midst." Looking at the older woman with a smile, "I was out bartering when Annie here caught my interest.

Annie looked around and with a crooked finger drew them close. She whispered they should not be here, but the best flowers bloomed in this place and she kept her pretty treasures within. "The lady would not mind," she whispered.

Myst thought the old woman daft and was about to leave, but Willow pulled her to the side. "All is not as it seems," she said, in whispered voice. Beautiful flowers grew wild all around this rocky area. Seeing Myst's doubt, she motioned her to follow as the old woman disappeared through the wall.

"Here," was all she said, as she took Myst's hand and lifted the heavy vines. A large, rusty locked gate stood before them. Myst gasped seeing the old woman picking flowers inside the most beautiful wild garden. This had to be Aries stepmother's secret garden. Willow and Myst stood for a moment then looked to one another with large smiles.

"Well, no one has been through these gates in a very long time." Myst used her wand to break away the heavy vines wrapped all around the majestic gates. They stood for a moment in awe, before them stood Ariel's secret garden. Myst and Willow saw the tiny Annie picking her beloved flowers.

This garden had been well hidden within the palace walls, tucked into the back of the mountain, where the waterfall fed into the moat. There use to be a small paddle which, when swung into place, would feed a small creek that branched out though the garden itself, coming back together as one creek to dump into a well on the other side. It was mastermind architecture, watering the garden every day, though the garden, now clogged with rubbish, and no longer worked. They followed the indications of the creeks that were just ruts of dust where the veins of water should have been converging into one larger waterway running under a beautiful stone step-bridge. This was why the moat was now murky with mud and motionless.

How Myst or anyone for that matter could, have completely missed this place? Tucked within the palace walls, covered now in overgrown roses, moss and weeds, this secret garden would be the perfect wedding setting for the couple. The people knew it forbidden by Alyas, but not the new King, he was as clueless as the rest of its location.

It was Annie's turn to startle them out of their enchantment as she whispered, "Maybe you could convince the new King to let us back in?" Annie gazed at the two of them, hope in her eyes, awaiting an answer.

Willow broke this silence with a low, "Let's do it!"

Gossip spread quickly of the wedding in the old garden and the new Queen to be was not to know, however, the sorcerer needed a lot of help. The elders, remembering this enchanted place, eagerly grabbed what was needed to help in the cleaning. But, as the group stood at the sagging gates, they were sorely disappointed; they gazed around in this withered garden, shaking their heads at the mess. They had no idea where to even begin. This garden would need a miracle to be ready in three days. Myst, Willow and Odysseus assured the gloomy gathering it could be done.

Odysseus addressed the group about imagination, hard work and magick. It did not take long for the faces of simple farmers and crafters to light up with a new sense of hope. They rallied around and established the need for a foreman in each segment to oversee the garden.

They had worked hard, raking debris away, digging trenches free for new water flow, the smith working on the gates and water paddle that would allow fresh water to flow. Crafters were on the statues, they did what they could.

Standing there, they shook their tired, dusty heads. Myst saw the wrapped blistered hands. She passed out an ointment to all, assuring them they had done well. Myst and Odysseus saw their disappointment as they shuffled out of this over-run garden, once so beautiful with its shining stone paths and sparkling blue water.

Leaving, they heard his parting words. "Have faith; be here at dawn of this next day. I will show you this can be done."

That night, all the people were out contemplating the events of the day. A golden light suddenly cast over the lost garden, continuing on through the night. The villagers were curious, but none had the courage to peek within. Come time for sleep, everyone, including the children, dozed off with smiles. For the first time in a long time, they were excited, something was happening. They even arose early, barely able to wait the trek to the 'garden.' If they would have peaked in, they would not have believed their eyes, for there was a small girl and a golden dragon cleaning at a rapid pace. They sprinkled a golden dust all over this garden, which vanished into the stone, flowers, the very soil itself.

The Lady of the Garden, in her rightful place stood at the entrance, overlooking the garden, the inspiration.

They could not believe the accomplishments and admired the new garden. The Lady would be more than pleased with a garden in her name, with new twists and turns. The Lady use to tell fairy tales to the children around the fountain, now, even their offspring believed.

The people eagerly poured in through the now fixed gates, bowing to their Lady, who did seem to be smiling and watching. They watched as her eyes seemed to follow them. Eager to finish 'her' garden, they scurried about. The statues were pulled into place, the smithy put the final touches on the levers linked to the fountains and they instantly started to flow. The other paddle was freed and sparkling water spread into every ditch feeding every creek and pool. There were giggles from the children as they released their butterflies into the air; tears flowed from those who touched the statue, remembering this garden and its lovely Lady. For the first time since the loss of their Queen, things felt right and good again. The wedding place was a secret no longer, only Aries did not know.

The night before the wedding, Aries was bathed, oiled down and put into his 'new' robe of satin. It was hidden in his old trunk to 'accidentally' find, the robe had been secretly placed, with a loving tag, from Lotus. It was a private, thoughtful, gift.

Aries, with a stab of sudden guilt of what Amber had done to him, worried what may come of it. What would he do if a messenger showed telling him he need send a mid-wife? And where was that little minx hiding now? Should he tell his little sorceress what transpired or take Alex's advice and not tell her unless it was crucial? How would she take his disloyalty, or was it? He had not yet wed when the deed was done; then why did he feel this would break her heart? Because he knew if it was the other way around he would duel this other man to the death. She would be his and his alone.

Just the thought of a mate, a loving mate, made the night go so slow. He sat in front of the fireplace with a good, dark wine and his thoughts of Lotus. She said she had loved him for a long time. Why did he not notice her at a ball, or seen her in the palace? Aries would ask her later, for it made no sense to him now. She was too stunning to overlook or hideaway. He sat up in a jerk spilling wine over the fur rug. The spill reminded him of blood stained eyes; the blood stained eyes of Belisma! His mind whirled into a travesty of these new mixed thoughts and deep rooted feelings. Belisma's small, scared, child apprentice, who the wizard had constantly abused, always yelling at; that same child who never spoke. Always behind the wizard, hiding, just as she now hid within her cloak of gold.

The arrow that killed his father was for him; Belisma wanted no heirs to this Kingdom and wanted him dead. Somehow, his little Lotus had deflected the arrow away and then hid, not knowing what to do. He knew in his heart she meant only to protect him, not knowing this arrow would hit his Father.

Aries, assuming the poor child had gone with the evil wizard, never gave it another thought. Now as he thought on it, Myst had found an apprentice so soon after her arrival. Lotus must have come out of hiding when Myst arrived, probably practicing her magick in the empty west tower, all alone, afraid of him. It was only reasonable she would come to Myst, for she was a stranger, just as lonely.

It had something to do with her shyness, probably Belisma's constant barking. Aries' blood started to boil at the thought, wondering with heat and hate if the vile man touched her, beat her or worst yet . . . no, he could not allow his mind to wonder in the evil wizards secret desires. He would kill that foul weakling wizard with his own bare hands, his wine goblet exploded at the mere thought. He looked at his hand, undamaged, but could not say as much for the fur hearth rug as it soaked up yet more wine. He looked towards the hiss, like an evil snake, as wine splattered onto the embers still glowing around the fire.

Aries abrupt thought, Belisma's treatment of his soon bride, made him wonder at her magick. How was it she was his apprentice to begin with? Perhaps kidnapped, or was she family? He hoped not the latter. Lotus looked nothing like Belisma, but if kin, he would certainly never leave her now, would he? She must have hidden her powers from them all, learning, studying him without his knowledge, maybe hoping for the day she could overpower him and leave.

Lotus must have immense revulsion towards her teacher and with so called wizard Belisma. Thinking now of her all alone in the caverns, hiding from him and the people, made him feel like a brute, never giving her a thought. She was just a young urchin, picked from many child thieves, stealing food in order to feed families or friends. This small child, no, now young woman, could have done nothing to save his father. Feeling Lotus' sorrow in his own heart, he vowed to make her life a fairy tale from here on, just for loving him from afar.

CHAPTER 14

Aries and Lotus Wed

A small, vigilantly made, tunnel of vines and flowers, once dark and mysterious, became bright in gold as it glittered; then a light burst forth as if magically spilling out and around the people. The crowd stilled, shocked and amazed by the sight before them. They ducked with a cry of wonder and fright as the lights swooped, flooding between them and over their heads.

One brave old man stuck out a crooked finger, the light landed on it. One small orb flew to his cheek and gave, what felt to him, a small kiss, then went back to perch on his finger. His cloudy eyes cleared in an instant and he saw one of the wonders of the night, for it was a fairy which sat upon his finger. Her body slender, her hair shimmering gold, flowing in an unknown breeze, her transparent wings were like a butterfly flitting on the wind. She smiled her tiny smile, waved goodbye, and with a giggle of delight, left his finger. He watched her go back in the tunnel. This was only the beginning. A little girl, with a basket of rose petals, skipped out of the tunnel, sprinkling them everywhere. She threw some of the rose petals high, so the fairies could ride in the cup of the petal, then some almost to the ground before, with a giggle, they would push off in the breeze and catch another. It was grand fun for everyone to see this little innocent girl and fairies play.

"This, my friend, has the signature of a great sorceress to be," whispered Alex, into Aries ear. Aries waited patiently, amused and delighted by the display of magick, the wonder and joy of his people. In reality, he was in admiration of his bride's power, the fairies, the garden, even the statue, all this magick surrounding them, but now he had had enough magick, he wished to see his wife to be.

Nathaniel watched with pride as Vickie emerged from the tunnel entrance. She was beautiful, in her dress of translucent layers. Her hair braided within three colors. She looked like the fairy princess herself.

"Is this my sister which I saw climbing a rope a couple of days ago?" whispered Alex, to Nathaniel, as he smiled and slapped his knee. Alex was suddenly quiet, receiving a jab in the ribs from Nate. Aries and Nate smiled at a now uncomfortable Alex, as Odysseus tried very hard to hide his smile.

Aries then turned to them both and asked, "Was she really climbing a rope to enter my palace?" Aries was very amused, but looked troubled at the same time.

"She has many talents," whispered Nathaniel, now irritated with Alex, but not for long.

Vickie walked the path over the bridge, climbing the few steps into the pavilion with the rest. She smiled sweetly to Nathaniel, his knees went weak. Vickie then turned and nodded all was in the ready. She raised her hands for all to stand for their new Queen to be. They stood tall, waiting for the bride. The tune changed; out stepped the surprise, the vision they had waited for.

There at the entrance appeared a gold caped woman with large hood. Nothing of the bride's features could be seen through the veil. Fairies swirled around her, lifting the cape slowly to reveal a golden goddess, their destiny.

The audience held their breath as the cape came off. The bride to be lifted her arms, tipping her head back, so the cape slipped off with ease. Her arms slowly lowered, as did her head, showing all her beauty.

Aries grabbed hold of Alex's arm with one hand; the other hand went to his chest. Aries was held spellbound. The audience silent, riveted to the beauty before them.

She stood before them in white floating satin and looked to be dipped in gold dust. The dress was low cut, almost too low for Aries taste. He saw the gazes of the young men. The gown had long sleeves, so full they touched the ground, trimmed all round in golden ruffles, gold piping and garnet jewels. Gold jewelry of a sorceress, binding her as protector to this palace, she was the vision of beauty itself. The fairies played in her bouquet of red passion roses, pink baby's breath and fern that trailed to the ground. Fairies carried the fine thin velvet train of her gown, as she glided down the cobble stone path towards her new husband. She hesitated on top of the footbridge, all waited to see if she changed her mind. Everyone would remember her as a golden dream, as her silken hair lifted in the breeze, exquisite beyond compare. She raised her hand; water could be heard from the mountain. It rushed towards her, filling all the dry creeks and pathways. She stood there as water rushed under her feet, making a complete circle, filling the well. Lotus then turned, and with a radiant smile to the King, completed her path.

Lotus put her small hand out to Aries; he helped her up those last few steps to stand beside him. Aries looked down at her small hands, fearing he would crush them with just a squeeze. Looking to her small waist, he realized his hands could go all around her; she was to protect him and the kingdom?

Odysseus, as new wizard of the palace, said few words. They each took a candle and lit the single one alone in the center, showing they were now two different people, blending their lives into one. Then, facing each other, hand holding of love, Odysseus leisurely wrapped the golden cord around their wrists. Now, bound to the other, they told each of their love and swore their fidelity. They then kneeled before Odysseus, as he placed the new matching gold and garnet crowns upon their heads, one by one. Odysseus, turning them to the crowd, pronounced them King and Queen of the White Sands. As if on cue, a sparkling beam of sunlight hit both crowns, as if the heavens proclaimed them as well. Everyone cheered for their first kiss.

Aries bent low, as Lotus rose on tiptoes, for a kiss. After many giggles, Aries gently turned and dipped her low on bended knee to give her the wedding kiss, a kiss that would seem not to end. He let her up to cheers, happy tidings, and a very red faced Lotus. The King then invited all inside the main hall for food, drinks and merriment, as the rest stood to give hearty handshakes and hugs of well-wishes. The old man made his way to Aries, shook his hand then, still, with tears in his eyes, turned to congratulate this stunning bride. He was quite surprised when she hugged him tight and kissed him on the cheek.

"I know you miss the Lady, maybe I can help a little," she whispered. "You worked hard to make this possible and you were rewarded. Your eyesight is much better, yes?" Before he could respond, he was rushed to move on so the person could congratulate the new couple; leaving him to be led into the main hall for the feast of his life. He looked back at her smiling face with love, an aged finger touching his face where she had kissed him. His eyes shone with the bright adoration of a pup, instead of a tired old dog. Everyone entered the palace washed their hands in a shower of mist to clean, cool, and give a sense of mystery.

Alex entered, shouting, "Myst, this is the last of the crowd, be damned if I will be seeing you now!"

"As if by wishful thinking my loud friend," Myst replied with irony, appearing behind a still damp struggling Spyder. "Here I am with a friend of yours who thinks he's allergic to water. I hear he gave them a terrible time with a bath," she whispered to Alex, pushing Spyder forward.

Spyder heard this comment and had one of his own. "Milord, ya should have seen the situation ya left me with. I was outnumbered, but I fought valiantly."

"We'll talk about it later," Alex, trying hard to hide his laugh, gruffly said.

The bride and groom sat on the raised dais, toasting long lives and happiness, with old friends and new. The time was getting late. Lotus, reluctantly, pried from her groom, had to be readied, prepared for her new room, her first night, with Aries. She would be staying, sleeping in the royal chamber with her new husband and King, giving Odysseus the west tower as his own room for the nights. In Aries' rooms she was to be bathed, readied for her new husband. Lotus' nerves began to betray her, the chamber too much, too large to be alone. Spyder was not the only one to fight valiantly for a private bath, for Lotus was much too shy for people to see her nude. She sent all, but one servant, away while she quickly bathed, attended to the whole time from the shadows. After her bath the servant was relieved of her duties, to inform his Lord she was ready.

Lotus spied a large wrapped gift on the bed, the tag signed by Odysseus & Myst. What could they have conjured? Aries would not mind if she opened this one without him. On opening, her breath caught, her nerves replaced by excitement! Lotus would be able to tell Aries he was King by right. That they had known each other long ago when she worked for Belisma; how was he going to take this news? She worked for the dark wizard who destroyed his life, their life. To have heard of this wizard's evil deeds, even committing murder, twice, to his family, yet, she had been so small, she could do nothing.

Belisma was a boaster of his deeds and they sickened her. When she found his intention was to kill Aries, fulfilling his prophecy of greatness, she decided to make her stand, her one disastrous stand. Lotus could not concentrate on her magick and her timing was off. Belisma had beaten her then for her interference, but she did not feel it. She felt she had deserved it, for the arrow had missed Aries, but hit the King instead and she knew he would die. Lotus had searched frantically for an antidote to Belisma's poison, but in such a great hurry to leave, he had left her little to study.

She knew his books and studies were anxiously, but carefully, packed, leaving her nothing. She knew he took the cure with him, she had seen it once, long as it was, and he always carried his book with him.

While Lotus was upstairs wrestling with her demons, downstairs was a bored, ready to be with his new bride, Aries. Toasts after toast were made until he chimed in, "Nathaniel, you might as well start, you're married and have twins, what's the secret?"

"Well, Milord, it wasn't an easy task, but we did manage," commented Nathaniel. This was met with many cheers and pats on his back, as Aries staggered away, the wrong way, in search of his bride.

Aries saw the maid coming for him. Batting at an unwanted attention with a slight smile, she made her way to the King and announced the Queen would see him now; he did not count on the announcement bringing assistance to his chambers. A horde of men, encouraging his luck, lifted Aries to their shoulders, jouncing him, as they carried him to his room. At the door, Aries demanded to be let-go and they did, at once, putting him on his unsteady feet, while trying to peer into the darkness of the room to see his new bride. Lotus, hearing the commotion from out the door, in fear, all but dropped their gift from the bed to cover her from peering eyes. Aries pried himself from the group of well-wishers, wedged himself between the wall and the door and then slammed the door against the mob. He leaned upon it as if he had just fought a great fight until he heard them leaving, grumbling, he sighed, making sure the door was secure and turned to see his new bride waiting patiently.

In Aries bed, all alone, but well covered from the fear of the mob. She was a vision beyond compare. Aries gazed upon the fire, the candles light, then to Lotus. The combination seemed to make her skin a burnished glow, and was almost too much for him. She dropped the blanket she used to cover herself from the others, at this, Aries jaw dropped as well. A sigh of relief came from her. There she was, in her signature gold, only this time it was see through. Candle light behind her, he saw every curve of her body. The fire light played in her hair, picking up the highlights from every strand, as it shimmered down to fan out over the bed. The dressing gown looked like fire itself. She faced him bravely, but the quiver of her body gave her away.

Aries was afraid for her, speaking to her softly, as with a child. It never crossed his slightly drunken mind, from all the toasts below, Lotus could be frightened of him. Will this little one burn him; his little Lotus, flower of his life. How could she fear him?

Another woman intended to frighten them all. Far away, one of the cloaked peasant girls, a witness to the wedding, slipped out of sight, to the forest, in a rage. Once in the forest she made her way to a well hidden path. She followed it carefully, for there were traps, until it ended at a hollowed tree. Under the moss covered bark, a hidden door. She looked around before she bent the false limb hanging from the tree and the door swung open. The tree was quite roomy and dry inside, with two small stones which lay at the base. She picked up one and it immediately started to glow, giving her enough light to see the hidden door at the far edge. She roamed with her hand, finding the latch, and picked up the small door leaning on the tree. She climbed down the ladder. In her anger she reached for a small rope, which was attached to the small door, yanked it and let it slam close. Never mind the dust rolling over her as she made her way down into the tunnel. 'Aries will pay for this,' she promised.

Amber always did as she was told. She could only fathom the visionary horror he would contrive for those not knowing his twisted ways. She shuddered as she hurried around and up the steps into a dungeon area. This large dungeon had a ghostly feel, with strange lights and sounds, and scared her when she was without him. She slid through the secret door to the stairs that would take her and her information to her master, for he had become more powerful every day as he lusted for revenge. He would see Lotus gone, King Aries under his power and her as Queen!

CHAPTER 15

The Wedding Night

Aries was afraid to move at first. Maybe this burnished beauty would take flight and he would find this all a dream, a terrible dream that would leave him all alone again, coming up with empty hands, the sands of time slipping through his fingers.

"I am not a dream," Lotus said, her voice dark and warm like sweet, dripping honey. "I am now your loving wife and have loved you my whole life, although, I must admit it has been a bit longer than you are aware of." She lowered her head in shame of what she had done in her past, all she had hidden from him, and now about to tell him. Her hair fell forward, her long lashes covered her eyes, making her look like a small child. "I should have told you all this before the wedding, but I feared your rejection."

Aries saw the glistening pool of a teardrop forming in her eye and, as if time were slowing, she blinked; Lotus' long dark lashes broke the teardrop like a spell. Now a glistening path made its way down, marring the perfection of her rose-colored cheek. He came to her quickly, not wanting to see the pain and torture in her eyes. Lowering himself to one knee at bedside, taking her tiny fragile hand, he brought it to his lips. Aries felt her tremble at his touch and was pleased. He was trembling as well. Aries brought out a gold ring with a garnet rose that sparkled in the candlelight, carefully placing it on her finger.

Lotus recognized it right away, she had seen it many times in the foyer, placed in a glass box. It was put there when Aries mother died, along with the rose garden. She knew the significance and felt unworthy, for he did not yet know of her dark side with Belisma. Feeling her guilt swell at all the things that she had seen this evil wizard do and the potions she had helped him make, Lotus was about to pull away. But upon seeing her hesitation Aries held her hand tight he said, "We had a lot of people decide that since you brought the garden back to life, you should have this." Aries looked into her eyes, amazed that it was a perfect fit, and he continued to calm her, "I think my father and stepmother would like for you to wear it and keep the gardens well.

Aries tried to start over, trying his best to tell her what he knew and how he knew her. "Lotus, when I saw you in my chambers, I was shocked to see a dream come true. A long time ago, I knew a child, we played in a meadow as princess and warrior. I never knew her real name, for we were always pretending, but I knew in my heart she would one day be mine. I went to meet her one day and she was gone, after a time, she became a dream. I mourned my loss, thinking you had moved on. Not knowing your real name, I could not ask the locals where you went, although I did look for you every day for awhile; then my mother died and I too moved on. I never did forget you."

Lotus was in shock. "You knew all this time, as I never spoke of it?"

"I was going to, then in minds eyes I saw this abused child of Belisma." At this her head snapped up in shock. "I wanted to help this child, but he kept this child well hidden within his robes. I had no idea it was you, my precious woman. If I had but known you were in need of my protection, "Milady what a fool I've been. Please forgive me."

"Forgive you? But you don't understand," Lotus said to him sadly. "I am the reason your father died." She pulled away from him and began to cry softly. "I learned of Belisma's plan to kill you at the hunt and could not tolerate to lose you that way. You had the right to see it coming and defend yourself, but with my meager talent, oh, Aries, I meant to send the arrow upward, instead it reflected off your armor and scratched your father. The dart was tipped with his special poison, I knew it would be a fatal wound. I was not strong enough to heal him, nor did I know anyone who could, accept Belisma himself. I begged him to heal the king, but he was in such rage and hurried state. I searched everywhere in the tower for the antidote to his vileness, to no avail. I knew he carried the cure in his book, but he carried it with him and I cannot remember the spell. I knew I was a failure as his apprentice, so I ran in despair to the caves, hid from you and from Belisma, in fear he would return. I cried for your sorrow, not knowing what to do, like the times before; he has done many awful things. About the time your mother died, Belisma came looking for you knowing the King would need his heir to carry on the name. This was long ago when we played in the meadow; I was early and eager to see you that day and was waiting in the meadow for you. Belisma came in a covered horse-drawn wagon, pretending to sell healing potions, herbs and such, but being from magick I saw through him and detained him. He asked too many questions of you. I had small powers you were not aware of and I felt the evil emitted from him. He was a dark wizard and I could not let him find my love, my warrior. I lied to him about wanting to learn more magick and showed him tricks I knew, luring him away from our meeting place. He seemed amused, then asked about you again. I lied once more, telling him a young boy I knew died of the fever with the mother that brought him. He seemed pleased and I left with him as his new apprentice, feeling that I had saved you. Please forgive me, I did it in love," Lotus pleaded. Her tears tore at his heart.

"What are you talking about? My mother was a peasant; Belisma didn't kill her," Aries protested, clearly perplexed.

"There is something you need to see." Lotus reached over to a cloth draped picture frame, and pulled the cloth free, Aries own eyes stared back at him in the face of the Queen. His hands shook, his mind reeled and with the implications of the picture. How could this be? He turned to Lotus in question.

"Seems the Queen's son was not stillborn after all, it was a lie for Belisma's benefit. She knew you were in danger, she gave you to her personal maid." Lotus lowered her dewy eyes to the picture. "She loved you enough to protect her only son and before she could have another; she was slowly poisoned."

"I am the true King?" His voice did not sound like his own, nor did his heart feel either, as it thundered in his chest and his ears. "I am not a bastard?"

"No, you never were. You are the true heir of this kingdom. It is I that does not deserve you, for I am the peasant from the meadow." She turned away from him, but he caught her small hand.

"Belisma is the one who must pay, not you, my love," Aries responded. "He is the one who stole my life and yours.

If not for three beautiful and meddling women; I would be dead. Seems my Mother and Queen loved me enough to lose me, a maid chose to love me as her own and a pretty girl risked her life for mine. I am a lucky man after all."

Looking into her eyes, she held his gaze, as he pushed her gently onto the pillows behind her. Lotus, mesmerized by his kind words, fell deep in blue pools of his passion filled eyes. His kiss soft, he slid one strap of the night-rail from her shoulder, like the feel of butterflies' wings. The other strap followed, as the form-fitting gown slid down her body. A flutter of anticipation flew through her body as he pulled her close. He heard the soft moan from deep within her, she felt limp and slowly relaxed against the pillows.

He followed her into the softness of the pillow placing a kiss upon her brow. Feeling bold, he softly kissed her neck. Lotus felt relaxed and pliant. He brought the kiss to her slightly parted lips. At first the kiss was soft, but Aries had been denied too long since Amber disappeared and felt the need to take what was his in his drunken state and pressed harder, more forcefully.

Only then did he hear, feel the fear and protest under his lips, as she struggled to stop him. What did he think he was doing? This was no concubine, no harlot, to just take any way he wanted. This was now his wife, to love, cherish, not rush. The girl in the meadow hid in fear behind an evil man. Which evil man did she hide from now as she covered her shoulders? He broke the kiss, left the bed; he had to clear his head. "I am sorry," Lotus, pleaded, "but I did tell you I was nervous."

Aries left her on the bed. She felt his intimacy drain as he walked from her. "I am so sorry," Lotus sobbed, thinking he was angry and disappointed in her.

"Don't be sorry." Aries smiled as he walked from behind the dressing screen with the matching garnet satin robes. He wore one, the other draped over his arm.

He held the robe for her and made a gesture for her to stand. Lotus, in her shyness, made him turn his head; he did so with a very large smile. Aries walked to the fire, a tiny Lotus behind him. He chuckled as he turned to see her standing there, hair ruffled, robe, much too large, wrapped around her, trailing behind, the sleeves covered her hands. He stopped and looked at her a moment and simply said, "My Priestess." They laughed. As she waited patiently, he arranged furs and pillows on the floor, sat in front of the fire with a carafe of wine, then looked to Lotus.

"Come to me. Let us snuggle in the rugs, drink of fine wine and see what happens, yes?" he asked, his eyes still shining with love for her.

She could not believe he could forgive her. He looked liked a tanned warrior that had somehow crept out of an old scroll and into her dream. She was amazed she had not had this vision as a dream. His waist long, blonde hair smooth, except for the braids common in the west region. The braids were small and only around the face. She had always seen herself in the shadow of someone great, never seeing the greatness in herself. Now, here she was, a sorceress and Queen to Aries, her long lost love. She liked the sound of his voice, deep with emotion, and the look of his magnificent body. He was not pushing, but taking time for her needs. She loved him even more for it.

They watched the fire. She edged to his side, shyly, ready to run at any time. Feeling good, as she became brave enough to sit close and actually snuggle into him. She felt good against him and they started to talk. Aries watched

Lotus' wine closely, filling when needed. They drank, then she hiccupped and they burst into laughter.

He asked about her life at the palace and then saw her face fall.

"Myst found me in one of the rooms she explored," said Lotus. "I was dirty and angry with what I had done to you and your father. I wanted to come to you, comfort you, but I was such a mess and only a throw off apprentice of Belisma's. You would have hated me for the things I saw and were involved in, but of little choice to keep you safe. I was in your room after the coronation, you looked so sad. I made a step, then saw Myst float into your room. I knew then, from that conversation, all would be well, though deep down in my heart, I knew I could never have you as my own. With broken heart, I returned to the caverns. I did not know, however, of Alex and his love for Myst."

Lotus told Aries of her magical transmutation, but not of the dragon. Odysseus and Myst knew she was already in love with Aries, she was still perplexed about it, but they knew. By then they were tipsy, warm and comfortable. Lotus was now even brave enough to play a game called 'Aura'. They sat close together and ran their hands around the other, without touching, trying to feel the other's emotions. The first one to touch the other, lost. They played for awhile until Aries touched her hair.

"You just lost," Lotus pronounced, her voice sounding breathless.

"Does it really matter now?" Aries asked.

"No, I guess not," she responded, with a soft smile. She spread her hands across his broad chest to feel the muscle and hair there. She heard the intake of his breath and realized she had some power over him as well. She became a little braver, sliding the robe off his shoulders.

With a growl, he pushed her into the soft pillows. The fire illuminated her hair and body, he wrapped her in his arms. "Enough games," he said, as he kissed her gently. Her brain told her to run, her heart telling her to stay, her wine filled senses told her she was his wife and Queen. "Love, I can wait for you no longer," Aries said, in a dark, warm voice. Aries saw her fear and regretted it immediately. He sat upon the pillows and furs and put his head in his hand, he look the bronzed statue of her dreams. "Lotus, I do not mean to scare you, but a man can only be teased for so long.

"Nor can I; she whispered." Aries felt a small trembling hand upon his shoulder. "Look at me, Aries, for now I am ready to learn, be a woman, and bear your heirs."

Aries expected to look up and see a cowering girl, instead, there she was, ready for him, and to do what it takes the first time to be a woman. He kissed her lightly, suddenly, they were on fire. Lovers at last, they caressed each other in liquid flames. The fire seemed to burn them, the flames entwining them together as man and woman. What happened to his shy girl? She had become the hellcat, her moans egged him on. They became intimate, intense. She pulled at his hair, scratched at his back. He was savage in his kisses, until they both lay limp, satisfied in front of the fire. Aries could not believe the little minx. They lay there for a time.

After awhile he picked her up and eased her into a tub. "We both need a bath to clean up and cool you off. I am a warrior and you are now the one that scares me." They laughed, splashed, played in the huge tub until the play becoming more romantic. They took their time, cleaned each other, stepped out and toweled dried. Aries brushed her hair in front of the fireplace until something caught his eye, long pale marks across her back. He practically yanked her back towards the firelight to see the fine lines that crisscrossed and marred her beauty.

"What is this?" Aries demanded.

"Myst and I have been working on them, soon they shall be gone, Milord, I promise," Lotus said with a smile, as if they were nothing of importance.

"They were worse?" He was furious. "Who did this to you, my love, and with what?"

"Oh, Aries, please do not do this. I think we both know. It is now behind us."

Lotus seemed unconcerned. Aries let it drop; continuing to brush her hair till it was dry and soft, like corn silk, with an unbelievable golden sheen running through his fingers.

Aries knew marks of the whip from abused horses, never from a woman. He would never forget who hurt his woman and would see to it he paid, many times over, for his many crimes. He loved this woman so; no wonder Alex was willing to put up a fight if he loved his Myst half as much as Aries loved this little flower. He scooped her up, carrying her stunning body to the bed. They lay in dim candlelight; but of no matter, for the sun was showing its face. They snuggled into satin and velvet, tired, satisfied, talking futures, new friends, the garden, the wedding of a lifetime, until they fell asleep in each other's arms.

A happy King, happy new Queen, a happy Kingdom.

CHAPTER 16

Packing and Leaving
White Sands

The next morning burst forth with a glorious light though the windows with beams of warming sun, piercing billowing white curtains and to shine on the Palace of White Sands. The rose color on the palace was now undeniable, standing taller, more majestic and impregnable. From the palace you could now see sails of fishing boats, as they jammed through waves, out for the days fishing. Lotus watched from her concealed balcony above the garden with mixed emotion. Aries lay, head in hand upon the bed, watching his new Queen, taking in the sights and smells. It was a permutation of sea air, roses and her. They had slept little, talking of their new future together. He felt her leave the bed, watched her walk enchantingly to the balcony, with just the sheet wrapped around her. The sheet trailed behind her, as she struggled to keep from tripping, but still, she was the Queen. He was not about to tell her, the sun shone right through her covering, as he viewed every curve of her body. Aries had to wonder how he managed to become so lucky. Seeing her hair flow long and free in the gentle wind, the sheet clinging her small frame, he could not help but smile.

"What is it you smile at, Milord King?" Lotus teased, as she approached him and then he noticed with quilt that she gently sat on the side of the bed.

"Good thing the balcony is on the back of this palace or my people would see my entire Queen," he teased. "We must rise, our friends leave today." Aries saw her fallen face, knowing their first night had fast become a beautiful memory. "We shall go visit, for Alex and Myst will be having their own their hand fasting soon enough." Aries was pleased at her smile as she dressed quickly.

Spyder walked in the garden, looking around carefully, having no clue the view he had just missed. Spyder walked to a vine covered wall, stood there awhile, then carefully pulled back the vines to reveal a small tunnel. He walked a short distance inside then plopped down on the cool grass beside Willow, who was feeding Sarpeden lumps of candied honey. Willow had shown him this entrance, knowing his fear of the dark. No one else knew of his fear. "Aries is going to be hoppin' mad when he finds out all these ways in and out of his own house." Spyder slapped a knee and looked to Willow. Willow gave a stern look. "Don't worry, I made out all the in's and out's of this place and gave them to Myst on the scroll, like ya told me to," Spyder said, with a smile. "It doesn't look like the same ol' castle as when we came in. I half feared goin' in the darn thing, cause it looked likely to fall atop my head, now 'tis sturdy."

Willow laughed. "It is not the same place. The rose quartz rock holding the castle together has more power now. Lotus and Aries loved each other so fiercely that it broke this awful curse. I've heard gossip of the West Lander's, and they did know of this curse; they're minds are now at ease." Spyder looked at her, shocked. She shrugged her shoulders and continued. "The people here knew something was wrong and it frightened them thinking Belisma still lurked about, or Myst was transforming their land, but now they know the real truth of the castles riddle; love within the castle has a strong influence. The stones crumbled, losing their vibrant color, but with the bloom of new love they filled once again with their rich, darker color, now holding the castle safe and secure." It makes sense to me, but I have no idea if it's true.

"And you know this how" he asked? Feeling a bit self-conscious she was so smart.

"I pay attention, silly." Willow tugged his ear in affection. Sarpeden laughed beside them. "I listen to legends people tell, things sorcerer's say, read stories written on walls, and most of all, converse with dragons who know a thing or two." Willow patted Sarpeden on the nose, then held a hand out for Spyder to help her up. "As lovely as it is here, I'm excited to be leaving for home today. Come, we must prepare Sarpeden for the trip. There is much to do." She pulled at a huge basket she wove from golden wheat stalks.

Sarpeden now seemed nervous. "Will the people fear me or try to kill me run from me?" It was obvious this large gold dragon feared the reaction of the people. Willows heart went out to her.

"We shall all be there with you to protect you my friend, for you are our ride home." Willow was very reassuring.

Lotus, Myst and Odysseus were going over last minute things. Lotus and Odysseus would have to work very close for him to learn the organization Myst had begun. Myst packed, readied her leave with a little remorse, when Odysseus noticed her book. Her eyes went straight away to her book, "It is the gift you sent to me," she confided. The one thing sorceress's are trained is to keep your book at hand at all times. "I hope you do not mind my altering it, for it has become unique for me and has seen some wear as well."

Odysseus reached for it, she gave it freely, with a smile. The book had changed in many ways.

What was once a plain thick leather book, was now thicker with new pages. Odysseus could see from the spine wear, she used it constantly. The older pages now tattered and somewhat stained, as every sorceress' books were. The leather now different, stamped in many colors by a great artisan. The blue of the waterfall and pond shimmered with lifelike depth and color, all surrounded by trees and branches, which swayed when you moved your head. Gold scalloped the edges, a pretty spell book, then he tried to open it. It was solid as a rock. Odysseus looked to Myst.

"Protected by magick? How do you open it my dear?" he asked, perplexed.

"The same way I disappear. I never reveal my magick, you taught me that yourself, Master," she replied, taking it back, holding tight under her arm. They giggled at Odysseus confounded face, until Aries walked into the room.

"A moment with you, Myst, if you please," he whispered pulling her out of the room, explaining the situation of the marks on Lotus' back. "I vow to kill that depraved man if I ever get my hands around his throat," Aries whispered in wrath.

"I promise all will be well. I will heal her," she whispered back. "Aries, I must tell you I have been treating her scars for quite some time. By the time I found her they were in sore condition. She was smart enough to heal some, but there were places she could not reach. This man is evil to beat a woman so, leaving her with wounds to treat herself. They were squarely placed, center of her back. He knew she dare not go for attention and left her to die in the caves." She had brought his fury higher, to the boiling point. Myst saw the vein on his forehead pulse. "The scars shall disappear and she now has you to protect her in the darkness. I can remove the physical look of the whip, but she does still have nightmares." Myst grabbed a large jar of cream with instructions that it must be applied every night. Aries nodded as he took the foul looking cream.

"You look ready to explode my boy," Odysseus said when they returned.

"It is personal business, my friend. I do, however, need a heavy drink," Aries dryly replied. He sat near the brandy and waited for his hate to dissipate. He watched Odysseus in amazement as he had two stacks of books already sorted and read just by running his hands over them.

Myst fought her own demons as she thought back to when she first saw the wounds Lotus had on her back from Belisma's beatings. Myst wanted to kill him. They were nasty whip marks, infected, while staying in that dirty lower level. Myst looked back in time, seeing Lotus as an animal. The herbs did help but Myst would never forget.

Unfortunately, there was no time to waste, on feeling pain, guilt, all must be readied to leave and soon. Myst and Lotus were finishing in their packing, when they however, found Aries and Odysseus had been celebrating for they were intoxicated. With a sigh and a curing drink, Myst was now the party masher of their fun.

Spyder, Vickie, Nathaniel, Willow, Alex and Myst were leaving that day while the weather was pleasant. They had been away from the North far too long, and Vickie especially was eager to return to her children. Aries held Myst's hands palm up and placed a kiss there. "I really don't know how to repay you for your kindness and the most magickal day of my life." Aries bowed to her.

"I do," Myst answered. "There is a sad creature tucked away, as Lotus was, in the caverns. It is within your power to release this creature to me."

"Name it," said Aries, with curiosity, "and the creature is yours."

"Thank you for your generosity," Myst responded, "for I name as my gift, Sarpeden, a golden dragon Belisma stole from its nest and hid within your castle walls."

Aries eyes looked as if they were about to pop with fear, as Aries whispered, "You say this creature was trained by Belisma, she must be evil by now and," Aries spat, enraged at being duped, "how could that man hide a dragon within these walls?"

Lotus stepped in. "Oh, Aries, let the poor thing go she is so unhappy. Whom do you think was feeding her? Myst and Willow love her, will care for her. If you must know everything there were two dragons down there, one good, one evil. Alexander and Nathaniel killed the red one before it escaped. Myst has a map that will show you all the entrances to your own castle, if you let Sarpeden go."

Aries could see he was out numbered, and did not want a dragon in the castle. He saw treachery in their eyes to get the map. "Be careful of dragons, they may turn on you. That is one thing my father did tell me," he said, fear in his eyes.

"I shall be very careful, do not be fearful," Myst assured him. "The golden one worked magick in your garden and made it what it is. The golden beauty comes from her, although my belief is the beauty is brought forth, from within, using kindness. As for my wedding gift to you . . ." Out of her sleeve came seven pair of water pixies, sliding into the water, down the waterfalls, out of the statues. She told the children there would be more, especially around ponds and creeks. Play with them when you can, but never harm one or they would return to her. The children nodded, running off to play with great delight.

Myst and Lotus walked with all people in tow to the now open garden to see the golden glow of Sarpeden with a handmade basket of straw that she could carry the group in with ease. "Are you sure this is safe?" Aries asked Lotus with great concern, seeing Willow holding on to what seemed a large dragon. "You should have seen the one we killed." Alex looked to Aries. They said their good-byes. Alex handed Aries a gift that looked like a tall bone cane.

"What you think I will age before my time?" asked Aries, at a loss.

"No," answered Alex. "Thought you would want a souvenir of the one we killed. It is one of his teeth." Aries almost dropped it. He could not believe there were dragons under his own feet. Aries walked towards the dragon with curiosity, trepidation.

Willow assured them Sarpeden was harmless and all spent some time feeling the scales and talking to her. The best part was feeding her vegetables and such. She was too young to breathe fire. There was no show of fear from the people now, for her golden glow was mesmerizing and charming. She had the power to change people for the good, was fire resistant and could swim like a fish.

Finally, the time to go was at hand. Willow said her good-byes, yet again, to Odysseus. With hugs and tears they mounted the glowing dragon. Odysseus, at the last moment, handed out gifts to all. From the depths of the palace came wines of great vintage, a special mirror for Nathaniel and Vickie. Nathaniel did not understand, but Vickie was ecstatic, telling him it was important for their family heritage. "Explain it at home, please," he whispered,

Spyder, now feeling the nobleman instead of the thief, asked permission to hand-fast with Willow. Seemed the quest had turned the little thief into a brave man. The group held their breath while Odysseus looked him up and down. The old wizard turned to Willow and asked if she had feelings for him as well. She nodded in her meek little way and permission was given. Odysseus patted Spyder on the back. "I am glad to be staying here awhile. You have yet to meet up with her mother," he said, as he lifted his daughter into the basket. The quest was over and they were on their way home, with promises to see each other soon.

Lotus gave Myst several books they had worked on. Myst looked to Lotus, simply saying, "The copy spell works well, don't you think?" They hugged again with more promises to see each other soon. Aries and Lotus would be coming to Myst and Alex's wedding.

Then, off they flew.

CHAPTER 17

❀

Captured Again by Belisma

They flew and swooped, laughed 'til they thought they would burst, except for Alex who looked a little pale. Myst went to him and made him drink of a vial of potion. "I was prepared for this," she explained.

Myst saw a huge and wavering city. It was far beneath a glittering sea of blue. She had a quick glimpse of this rare jewel, just off the shores of the Cel'eset arbor, a sight impossible to see from land. Myst drew a map of it in her book; she drew as fast as possible to get all the details. Magick seemed to protect it by a well rounded bubble of immeasurable size. Myst wondered at its buildings of immense shapes and pearl hues, intricate walls of sculptures well embellished with detailed shapes. It must be an ancient language on these gold wavering buildings, but could not begin to translate. She sketched what she could of the words written on the city walls then watched in amazement as people swam into portals then walked on legs into this magnificent city. When they entered the city, they seemed to be a race of people just like them, but dressed differently, more elaborate.

It was the most amazing magick she had ever seen. They looked to be merpeople of the stories Myst heard from bards and her ancestors as a child, but had never really seen one until now. Myst, living and loving the water, was captivated by these people, saviors of sailors in storm wrecked ships and such.

These were sensuous people, who glittered in the sunlight, another forgotten realm. Just as the Cel'eset's stories told to Myst as a child and she relished finding, living in the castle of the sea. She sketched everything she saw, wrote as rapidly as possible, hoping to get every element. Myst knew this was Alex and Vickie's homeland.

She was about to ask Alex about this extraordinary metropolis, if he had traveled though it or its natives before on one of his quests, when he unexpectedly turned to her.

"Myst, I cannot envisage something, especially from you, if you beyond doubt love me, as you say you do," he began, his eyes saddened. "Did you and Lotus try to impede us on this quest by sending out all sorts of creatures that were of the dark side of magick? I did not think either of you were capable of conjuring such things, such as the undead." Everyone looked at her with the same question.

Taken aback for a moment she answered, "But, Alex, we had no idea you were really coming. My mind was on home, yes, but I was exhausted. I was trying to get out of the wedding myself, by means of Lotus, for I knew she loved him. I sent no creatures to venture out to delay you, or to kill you. I could never do that. I love you all and you of all people should know that in your heart. Lotus and I both have the abilities to battle these demons, consequently, we learned the spell for counteract, but to do that . . ." she dropped the sentence and her head in horror. She could not, no, would not accept as true they would imagine this of her.

Everyone digested this new information. Myst was not capable of such monstrosities. They were thinking on who would be on the lookout to bring a quest party to bring to an end.

As if darkness suddenly appeared, a large shadow descended upon them. Sarpeden was a child compared to this dragon of dark. Its huge wing-span filled with translucent dark skin, separated with dark bones, each tipped by a lethal weapon of sharpened talon. The beast's back was prickly sharp, which contrasted with the oily black scales for a belly. Eerie eyes of moonstone blue

Alex had never seen a dragon so large and intimidating before. The almost white eyes on a black dragon were most hypnotizing. A puff of feathers topped its head, the end of his tail, and around each leg; his was the strangest dragon Alex had ever come across. They watched as his eyes fought to see his target. They were all in the ready. Alex and Nathaniel drawing swords, Willow with a spell of blinding light, Spyder with his short sword and Vickie with her grappling hooks. It was the woman in robes that was not ready.

"Myst, what are you doing? We are about to be eaten alive," shouted Alex, as he yanked her arm and spun her around.

"He's after my books," she shouted. As the dragon swooped and tipped the basket, his fangs showed, his eyes riveted on Myst. Alex, sensing the dragon's objective on Myst, drew his sword. Damn, when would he learn to trust the instinctual forewarning that something was amiss? Sarpeden dove, trying to dodge the enormous beast like a sparrow evading a hawk, but it was no use. Myst's books scattered all over the bottom of the basket, dropping them as the dragon's scaly claw knocked her out of the basket, then swooped down and plucked her out of the air, his claws wrapped around her waist as a gentle gem.

"Protect those books with your life and don't open them!" she screamed at Alex, over the sound of flapping dragon's wings. Drawing the dark dragons' attention back to the basket, the monster saw Alex pull his sword. As if to show this puny man he was no threat to him, the other claw bared a sharp talon, batting Alex away as though he were nothing, but not hurting him.

"Fine time to be distressed about the books now" Alex shouted in rage. He straightened himself up. Looking down, over the side of the basket, he had a majestic view of the land.

The dragon flew off, Myst in his claw, as everyone watched, helpless. The black wing span was amazing to them, but how could they fight him? The blinding light Willow shot at him was a total miss or simply did not affect him. Swords were useless and Myst had not been ready. Why did he target Myst?

Sarpeden, caught off guard, shook in fear, her golden wings trembling as she tried to maintain her flight. She almost dropped the basket. As it was, she just jumbled them around a bit. Alex grabbed the books and tucked them in his armor.

"Follow him" Alex commanded.

"I will follow from a distance, but he is far too big for me to battle," Sarpeden called out in flight. The black dragon flew, Myst still in his claw, for quite a distance.

"Did I hurt you Milady?" The beast finally spoke.

Her head snapped up in confusion, "No, you did not, but why was I taken" she asked, thrashing about in his grasp.

The dark dragon looked at her with unease and plainly replied, "I had no alternative, I am as much a captive as you.

If you would take the time to look down, you might desire to discontinue in your thrashing about. If my grasp does not hold, can you fly, Milady?" She looked down and decided to still herself, as she saw it a long plummet to the ground. How could a dragon of this proportion be held captive? She wondered, just as he dropped a confused Myst on to a balcony, where a bizarre man caught her, as if he were waiting for this offering of her.

"I did your bidding as told," the dragon said, as he sneered to this shadowy robed man. With his great wing span the dragon pushed off into the wind, towards the mountain range, leaving Myst with a sad look in the arms of a man who carried his prize within his tower of darkness. His dark robes billowed in breeze the dragon had created. Myst was livid as this man carried her petite frame in the interior of this massive tower.

"Why did you capture me? What do you want? What can I possibly do to help you and most of all, who are you" As Myst was rambling out her questions a familiar face appeared, Amber, Aries concubine.

Myst started once more. "Amber, what goes here? Who is this man that controls dragons and takes people as if they were an apple to just pick?" Myst stared Amber down, but she was not backing up, she was bold and with adoring eyes. The dark man turned and lowered his hood to show his beady, watering eyes. In a whisper dripping of wolves bane, Amber made the introduction. "Myst, I would like you to meet the Grand Master, Belisma."

Sarpeden released the basket and the group dropped to the bottom of this strange tower. Looking up they saw Myst struggling in the arms of a strange man.

Vickie was the first to speak. "Why is it she does not use her magick?" Everyone then turned, ready for yet another battle, as they heard the heated animal growl. Echoing off the walls of the tower, it sounded feral, no sound a human could make. No one dared say a word. Alex had just rescued her and now had to do it again. One quest to another, will it never end?

Everything around the tower was lifeless, no trees, no animals, just rubble, rocks and dirt. The sides of this massive black tower were smooth, shiny and flat. Above their heads they saw nothing but sharp, peaked tops, no doors, nor windows, just a balcony high above. There were a few cracks, but not enough to edge their way to the balcony.

"Find a way," commanded Alex. Everyone looked for a solution. There would be no discussions with Alex when he was angry and they all knew him well enough not to even utter a word to reassure him. Vickie kept feeling these walls.

"What are you doing?" asked Nathaniel, watching her scan the walls.

"I have seen this stone before in caves Odysseus has sent me to. It is not a rock; this tower is a crystal shard, as if it sprang right out of the earth itself. They are dark elemental shards; whoever controls this element can order it to capture your soul if it so pleases its Master. Whoever captured Myst is powerful indeed, making a pack with the dark side is a dangerous thing to do, but a fast way to gain power." Vickie lay upon the ground. "This is one of many shards, this is a peak of a sunken dark realm, I can feel the whole of a city deep within the earth. It is a dangerous place to be."

"Who would bring up this sunken city and why" Nathaniel casually asked?

"Belisma," said Spyder; "he needs revenge on the west and wanted power fast. Makes sense to me."

It made sense to them, too, as they examined the outer surface, frantically trying to find a way in to save Myst. They stood still as rock, hearing her screech from inside. "So, you are Belisma, you evil, vile, unspeakable excuse of a wizard! I should eradicate you myself, but I promised that delight to Aries."

"Enough, woman" Belisma shouted, waving his hand. Suddenly Myst could not move or talk.

Amber cowered at first, then came out in glee. This Myst was the woman she hated, that she wanted dead, but not as much as Aries' new bride. Her Master was growing in power. Soon, she would be Queen, with Aries doing her bidding while Belisma ruled. Amber just wanted to be Queen in title and wanted Aries badly, as long as she could dress the part and be served, she did not care. Down below, the sudden hush of Myst moved the group to come up with a quick plan. Sarpeden would make an arch and drop the group off on the balcony. Then she and Willow would hide in the nearby forest, until they could free Myst. Sarpeden and Willow were also in charge of Myst's books. Myst had all her most powerful spells in those books and she would not want them in the hands of an evil wizard.

Spyder pulled Willow to one side and whispered, "I know it's not much, but if we don't get out of this, I want you to have me bag." Willow looked in and saw all his treasures acquired on this quest. She was touched.

"I will look after them for you, but I will see you again and soon, for I feel it in my heart. I have a little magick of my own and you will be fine." Then Willow kissed him full on the lips. Everyone saw, not a soul said a word.

Sarpeden placed them with stealth, making not a sound, but they were not ready for the iron gate that dropped, covering the opening in front of them. All saw Myst floating parallel in some kind of trance, about two feet off a stone table; dark webs were being wrapped around her body by wisps of the undead. The little spider creatures wound around her, covering her in sparkling dark webs, completely, as if a spider would a cocoon. They would confuse her mind, bend her will, make her forget; Alex knew them from the darkness of some of the caves. He roared in frustration, reaching through the gate for her, straining, as if his strength and will could bend the bars. Alex yelled out to Myst, "If you love me and want this life with me, you must fight the darkness that weaves within your mind." The man with her smiled at Alex, then, with a wave of his hand, a smooth wall fell in front of the gate, almost taking Alex's arm off, and they could no longer see her. Alex slammed his hand against the now flat barrier.

"If she fights . . ." Alex began. He knew these creatures, saw her weakened condition. He looked if all was lost.

CHAPTER 18

Belisma

"I have never, ever, seen my brother give up and I do not intend to now. We storm the tower," Vickie shouted at the wall, "to bad Morgan is not here, your mighty steed seems to be missing out on this one," Vickie giggled to Alex. "She is a powerful sorceress, Alex, she knows we are all here waiting, she will now allow herself to succumb to this evil, you know that."

Vickie looked sternly to Nathaniel as he blurted out, "What are we going to do now? We have no wizard and our sorceress is already inside." Nathaniel looked panicked as he cast his worried eyes toward his wife.

"Well, couldn't get much worse," Spyder said, shrugging, leaning on the bars.

Just then, the small balcony they were huddled on started to slide in towards the tower, at the same time the Iron Gate slowly began to pull up, now leaving them nothing to cling to but a smooth wall. Panic ran from one to another.

"Just had to go and shoot your mouth off," Vickie slapped him on the back of his head and looked at Spyder with a smirk, trying to get her composer back.

"Well, I am going to wrap my hook and rope around the gate before it disappears. If I had a magick sword, or dagger, I would be wedging it in there as well and see how long I can hang before I drop to my death!" she announced to the wall quite loudly.

The group flew into action wedging objects into the gate as it pulled them off their feet and the balcony disappeared beneath their feet. They hung there long and hard, even Spyder found a toehold and held onto the rope with Vickie. When they thought all was lost, the balcony made a small sound and sneaked out enough for a foothold as it reappeared. Little by little the balcony started to reappear. It snaked its way out as if in an effort or if the evil within wanted them to trust it enough to let go and then it would quickly slide back in. The group looked at each other in suspicious reprieve.

Alex hoping that Myst had fought the darkness after all and heard their cries for help, it maybe was her way of extending the balcony enough to save them for awhile to climb down and escape without her. Then again it could be a cruel trick to have them let down their guard. Alex told everyone to hang tight, just in case. It was then that they heard a dark, sinister voice say, "you might as well come in now, my friends, you are just hanging there, I just hate to be interrupted while I am working."

The wall slid up slowly at Belisma's command. He and his small companions were well into the interior of this odd room. The dangling group holding desperately in the wind, now looking silly, but obviously stunned by what they saw, it was not a slow decision on any ones part to jump into the room before this lunatic changed his mind. None of them had a death wish. Inside this massive room stood the evil Belisma himself and one stunning and strangely dressed woman, this woman was dressed in bell sleeved luxurious, deep red, dark satin. Gold trimmed piping accented her dress. She dripped in jewelry, and gold was weaved into her hair.

"Amber," bellowed Alex, "What goes here?" Everyone looked to Alex.

"You know this thing? This is the woman that spread the gossip of Myst and her dark deeds of the west tower? Vickie hissed in his ear.

"Yes," he replied. "She is the one and only, Dancer and concubine of Aries' palace. It seems she was spreading her lies and legs for this pathetic worm as well. Her talents seem many."

Amber glared at Alex and started, "and if we were not interrupted for the meeting of Aries wedding arrangements, I would have wrapped you around my little finger as well," Amber ended with an up-held hand, extended pinky finer at him. "Alyas sent me to serve you in every way, was his son that chose to keep me for himself. I know he loves me and I shall rule as queen, Belisma will see to it as my reward!"

Alex was appalled; as was the rest, "you cannot be serious? Have you not seen him with his new bride? She out-shines you as the sun does the moon. He will never give her up for you."

"He will if she is dead and there is a spell upon him to love me. Belisma can rule the white sands and Aries and I shall reign as King and Queen," Amber spit out.

Alex stood straight and started, "Amber as long as I draw breath that will never . . . ," Alex looked down at his chest to see Nathaniel's hand restraining him; he had not realized that as he spoke he was also taking steps towards his destination.

With a pleading look Nathaniel whispered, "Take another path or we breathe our last breath, my friend. It is now time for you to think with your head and not your heart."

Alex retreated with the rest, but he could not help in his concern to demand, "Where is my Myst and what do you want with my woman?"

"Oh, I'm afraid she isn't yours anymore," the rodent-like man sneered. "I've put her under a rather nasty little spell that I learned long ago, if you happen to know dark magick and you happen to stumble into one of the forgotten realms of the black shards. With a little of their teaching I have become more powerful for a price, but in a short amount of time and gold is now not an issue as I have learned to have others work for me as what you would call collectors. I simply sit here, collect my gold, give my workers their cut and as I said before, gold is not exactly a problem."

"I have seen this dark magick before, with these creatures that look as spiders that sparkle in the dark. I know them to be dark weavers of magick, I have fought them before and I ask you once again, what it is you want of my woman." Alex was becoming enraged and this was not a good sign for the rest.

"And as I told you before, this is no longer your woman anymore, warrior, now she is my sorceress, for I am the great dark wizard and she will work with me, and take care of my every wish. She is night mistress, beautiful, distinctive, and shimmering for my taste, not yours."

Belisma waved his hand and a slice of black shard opened to reveal a new Myst. Alex watched in disbelief as Myst appeared in a tight black and red outfit, the top was short, showing her stomach, low-cut, with long sleeves that came to a jagged point. The skirt slit almost to the waist and her hair was weaved in red tinsel. A black snake with red eyes, made of metal hung at her forehead. She looked like evil itself. Belisma stood on a pedestal, looking like a tall black rat in a fine black cape, with black leather boots accented with silver straps. For the rodent he was, he did dress well and with a woman on either side of him, majestic indeed.

Vickie closed Spyder's mouth, as they entered even more into Belisma's domain. Spyder had been staring at Myst as if he'd never seen her before. Wary eyes glanced at Myst and the little man beside her was she really completely in his control? Then they noticed movement; the shadows moving, a black cauldron bubbled with a swirling gray fog emanating from it.

Everything was dark, gray and dismal except Myst and Amber.

As Belisma reached up and ran a slimy hand down Myst's hair. Alex noticed her shudder of revulsion. Just maybe she had fought it off successfully, but Alex knew the chances of that were slim at best, she went in exhausted.

"It was I that tried to turn you back, it was my creation of monsters, although I did not know at the time that Amber here, had hired the witches, I just gave them a more powerful place to live and more power to fight you with. That gave you only a small taste of my powers," Belisma boasted.

Alex could not believe that Myst just stood there listening to this rat. Her eyes caught his, and something flickered there, a desperate plea for understanding. She was begging him with her eyes to see something important, but what?

Belisma put a finger under Myst's chin and whispered in her ear. It was almost more than Alex could bear before he tore the man's throat out!

"He has learned much and in a short amount of time. He seeks revenge on you and now with me by his side; you stand no chance against us," Myst avowed as a matter of fact.

"Good, my dear. This is exactly what I want from you, and you will remain so pliant, or your friends die one at a time," he hissed at her, grabbing her arm and yanking her close. Alex jaw tightened at his oily touch on her and seeing the fingertip bruises that would darken her fine porcelain skin where he had grabbed her.

"I understand, Master, and will do your bidding, for none of these people are a threat to us. They mean nothing to me now and besides, this group contains no magick without me," she turned to sneer at Vickie,

"No real magick."

Alex took a step forward, but Nathaniel threw his arm in front of him. "We need to keep our wits about us man, or we die, and so does Myst."

Alex took a step back. "Fine, we do that, my friend," Alex answered Nathaniel with a sneering smile towards Belisma.

Vickie almost smiled, picking up Myst's cryptic signal. "No magick here," she confirmed, but Myst knew better. She was trying to tell them something. Perhaps she wasn't really under Belisma's spell, not completely. She loved Alex with all her power and before they disappeared behind the wall he had yelled out to her to fight the darkness.

Vickie waited the opportunity with a cat smile-seemed Myst might have a plan.

Alex asked casually, "You are the man that killed Aries' father and mother as well. You keep pretty company for a murderer."

"They were in the way of my dreams and I did not care for the old man, but the arrow was meant for the young buck Aries. If he were to wed and have heirs, then I could not control what was mine, my apprentice stepped in the way and made a mockery of me. She paid for that, though, as I beat her almost to the death and then left her. I knew she would get no compassion from the nobles or the locals. I saw to her death."

Vickie gave a warning glare to Alex, Belisma did not know that Louts has survived and had married Aries, he would be livid if he knew.

Alex was now worried what this mad man had in store for them all and could not help being protective of his woman. His sword sang with his temper and he growled at the man that kept them apart once again, as his rage flared. Myst tried to shake her head "no," but Alex didn't notice in his frenzy, though the others did try to hold him back.

"I tried to warn you, now you are on your own. We will not all die because you cannot hold that temper of yours." Nathaniel let him go with an apologetic shrug to a wide-eyed Myst. They all knew that she was not there when his powers showed them-selves and were sworn to secrecy by Alex in case she would no longer love him, against their better judgment.

"This is not allowed," Belisma squeaked, almost being panic-stricken by this large warrior. In an elaborated movement, he clutched at a staff. "I need a new statue by my throne. This is the man who desires you?" he asked of Myst knowing it to be so.

Before Myst could even try to stop him, he threw a great ball of gray flame at Alex. Alex dodged the flame as the others leapt backward into the corner. Alex pulled his sword and ran toward the evil wizard with death intended. Belisma was ready for him, though, and with another wave of gray flame and Alex being closer now; the flame hit Alex straight to the chest. Alex stood still as if frozen and looked to a helpless

Myst. If Myst gave away herself now, all of them would be lost, and so she stood as the others and watched in horror as cold marble started to creep up Alex's legs, engulfing him in stone.

Belisma laughed as Amber squealed in delight. With a wave of his staff, he then levitated the marble Alex to a corner by his throne made of black shinning crystals with a skull on each peak. Alex now stood with a crystal sword, in hand, as the rest watched, for his revenge would come.

"He is not dead, you all know, just tied up for a very long time" Belisma was pleased with him-self and turned to Myst. "Is there anything I missed my dear?" As Belisma studied the new statue, "anything you would decorate him with?"

Myst laughed, "Yes, Master, he always carried this to remind himself of me, he can have it now." Myst walked to the statue and placed a bluish tinted bracelet with feathers on it, she wrapped it carefully around his hardened finger and whispered knowing he could hear, "you fool, you complicate things, I shall figure this out. Watch for the glow in these feathers and be ready."

"Now Alex is a mere statue of gray with the last of my possessions. I am done with him."

"And for the rest of your friends: I want you to form a cage" he smiled at her. "Make it good. Make the kind you know I like. Now would not be a good time to displease me, now would it, with your lover stuck over there? He pointed to the far wall, "Where an eye can be kept on them."

Myst did as was told, as she formed a cage with her staff, the bars red and glowing, which they all knew death when touched. She placed it in the corner close to the doorway with a few stones on the ground within the bars.

Only Spyder would notice the plain lock on the cage that did not sparkle poison red like the rest and it was turned so he could pick it easily from with-in. Then they could use the rocks throwing them against the door to open it, easy enough. Spyder's face lit up as she made it. He nodded to her and then looked away. He knew, that was a relief, but she had to get everyone out of the room for the escape. He inspected the lock on his way in the cage.

Vickie was thinking when Myst's plan came into her head. Their eyes locked.

"Where is my book?" Myst wind whispered to Vickie as she closed the door to the cage with a wave of her hand as if they did not matter. "And just think it, don't speak. I shall play his game for a while, until I can stir Odysseus and Lotus, do you understand?" Vickie nodded.

Myst was relieved knowing her books, Willow and Sarpeden were safe.

Myst concentrated for a moment then smiled at Vickie; Lotus and Odysseus will help us for I've asked for their help. They should be awake soon, and indeed, Lotus was the first to hear her cry for help.

I was raised on a small farm in Ohio. Born in 1958 and spent many days with loving parents and Grandparents. As an only child, with many imaginary Creatures: I never grew out of this imaginary world of wonder.

I had my chores without pay and never asked —that was just the it was. Hay bailing, manure spreading, etc.

Life was simple. I did fall in love in high school and thought he was my soul mate-I was a fool; So, after all those years of searching for that perfect love and that perfect job, and even going to College for awhile at Sinclair. I still never felt like was one of the crowd, I decided to marry. I am now a widow losing him to cancer in 2000 and so I decided to close down.

It was then that I too became ill and slightly disabled, leaving me with the one thing that I knew I could do—write, with the flair of imagination. Therefore, here you have it, a "young" widow, and dreaming my big dream. I will always remember my grandparents and their teaching me of the old ways. I have met my many frogs and never found my Prince. I still dream, hope and sometimes cry at the adventurous/romance scenes. My true romance comes from writing fantasy which is my escape from my everyday life: striving on to prove that everyone can overcome their oppression and depression in their lives; as I now created the men of my dreams and the women I wished to be. I shall always be a hopeful romantic/adventuress in an overpowering world.

Also written by Victoria Morrow
The Quest for Myst-Book one of "The Colors of Magick"

Long ago, confusion seized the common folk as magickal creatures wreaked havoc upon their world by introducing magick the people did not understand. Kingdoms were torn apart as evil wizards took over. Now, the peaceable people with delicate magick are being hunted and drained of their powers. They must bring down the imposing evil forces if they hope to restore peace and calm in their land.

The prince of the commoner's realm, Alexander of the North, thought he had escaped this darkness until the death of his mother made him a warrior—and a hero with a dark secret. Even worse, he's prone to making mistakes. Promising his sister, Victoria, that she would be the new princess of the West is his first mistake; the second is falling in love with Myst, a fair maid from a misty pool. But Myst is more than just a peasant and has power beyond those of the mighty wizard for whom she is an apprentice. When Myst sacrifices herself to save the kingdom from war, Alex gathers an incredible group of people to save her from the clutches of evil.

But will Alex's powerful secret come back to haunt him?

I was so taken in by Ms. Victoria's prose/storytelling abilities.